by night
in chile

Also by Roberto Bolaño

AVAILABLE FROM NEW DIRECTIONS

Roberto Bolaño

by night
in chile

Translated by Chris Andrews

A NEW DIRECTIONS BOOK

Originally published by Editorial Anagrama as *Nocturno de Chile* in 2000. Published by
arrangement with the Harvill Press, London

Manufactured in the United States of America
New Directions Books are printed on acid-free paper.
First published as a New Directions Paperbook (NDP975) in 2003.

Library of Congress Cataloging-in-Publication Data
Bolaño, Roberto.
[Nocturno de Chile. English]
By night in Chile / by Roberto Bolaño ; translated by Chris Andrews.
p. cm.
ISBN-13: 978-0-8112-1547-3
1. Chile—History—1973–1988—Fiction. I. Andrews, Chris. II. Title.
PQ8098.412.043N6313 2003

2003013223

15 14 13 12

New Directions Books are published for James Laughlin
by New Directions Publishing Corporation
80 Eighth Avenue, New York 10011

for Carolina López and Lautaro Bolaño

"Take off your wig."

CHESTERTON

by night
in chile

I AM DYING NOW, BUT I STILL HAVE MANY THINGS to say. I used to be at peace with myself. Quiet and at peace. But it all blew up unexpectedly. That wizened youth is to blame. I was at peace. I am no longer at peace. There are a couple of points that have to be cleared up. So, propped up on one elbow, I will lift my noble, trembling head, and rummage through my memories to turn up the deeds that shall vindicate me and belie the slanderous rumors the wizened youth spread in a single stormlit night to sully my name. Or so he intended. One has to be responsible, as I have always said. One has a moral obligation to take responsibility for one's actions, and that includes one's words and silences, yes, one's silences, because silences rise to heaven too, and God hears them, and only God understands and judges them, so one must be very careful with one's silences. I am responsible in every way. My silences are immaculate. Let me make that clear. Clear to God above all. The rest I can forgo. But not God. I don't know how I got on to this. Sometimes I find myself propped up on one elbow, rambling on and dreaming and trying to make peace with myself. But sometimes I even forget my own name. My name is Sebastián Urrutia Lacroix. I am Chilean. My ancestors on my father's side came from the Basque country, or Euskadi, as it is now called. On my mother's side I hail from the gentle land of France, from a village whose name means Man on the Earth or perhaps Standing Man, my French is failing me as the end draws near. But I still have strength enough to remember and rebut the wizened youth's affronts, flung in my face one day, when without the slightest provocation and quite out of the blue, he appeared at the door of my house and insulted me. Let me make that clear. My aim is not to stir up conflict, it never has been, my aims are peace and responsibility for one's actions, for one's words and silences. I am a reasonable man. I have always been a reasonable man. At the age of thirteen I heard God's call and decided to enter a seminary. My father was opposed to the idea. He was not absolutely inflexible, but he was opposed to the idea. I can still remember his shadow slipping from room to room in our house, as if it were the shadow of a weasel or an eel. And I remember, I don't know how, but the fact is that I do remember my smile in the midst of the darkness, the smile of the child I was. And I remember a hunting scene on a tapestry. And a metal dish on which a meal was depicted with all the appropriate decorations. My smile and my trembling. And a year later, at the age of fourteen, I entered the seminary, and when I came out again, much later on, my mother kissed my hand and called me Father or I thought I heard her say Father, and when, in my astonishment, I protested, saying Don't call me Father, mother, I am your son, or maybe I didn't say Your son but The son, she began to cry or weep and then I thought, or maybe the thought has only occurred to me now, that life is a succession of misunderstandings, leading us on to the final truth, the only truth. And a little earlier or a little later, that is to say a few days before being ordained a priest or a couple of days after taking holy vows, I met Farewell, the famous Farewell, I don't remember exactly where, probably at his house, I did go to his house, although maybe I made the pilgrimage to the newspaper's editorial offices or perhaps I saw him for the first time at his club, one melancholy afternoon, like so many April afternoons in Santiago, although in my soul birds were singing and buds were bursting into flower, as the poet says, and there was Farewell, tall, a meter and eighty centimeters, although he seemed two meters tall to me, wearing a gray suit of fine English cloth, handmade shoes, a silk tie, a white shirt as immaculate as my hopes, gold cuff links, a tiepin bearing insignia I did not wish to interpret but whose meaning by no means escaped me, and Farewell invited me to sit down beside him, very close, or perhaps before that he took me into his library or the library of the club, and while we looked over the spines of the books he began to clear his throat, and while he was clearing his throat he may have been watching me out of the corner of his eye, although I can't be sure, since I kept my eyes fixed on the books, and then he said something I didn't understand or something my memory has not retained, and after that we sat down again, he in a Chesterfield, I on a chair, and we talked about the books whose spines we had been looking at and caressing, my young fingers fresh from the seminary, Farewell's thick fingers already rather crooked, not surprisingly given his age and his height, and we spoke about the books and the authors of the books, and Farewell's voice was like the voice of a large bird of prey soaring over rivers and mountains and valleys and ravines, never at a loss for the appropriate expression, the sentence that fitted his thought like a glove, and when with the naïveté of a fledgling, I said that I wanted to be a literary critic, that I wanted to follow in his footsteps, that for me nothing on earth could be more fulfilling than to read, and to present the results of my reading in good prose, when I said that, Farewell smiled and put his hand on my shoulder (a hand that felt as heavy as if it were encased in an iron gauntlet or heavier still) and he met my gaze and said it was not an easy path. In this barbaric country, the critic's path, he said, is not strewn with roses. In this country of estate owners, he said, literature is an oddity and nobody values knowing how to read. And since, in my timidity, I did not reply, he brought his face closer to mine and asked if something had upset or offended me. Perhaps you have an estate or your father does? No, I said. Well, I do, said Farewell, I have an estate near Chillán, with a little vineyard that produces quite passable wine. And without further ado he invited me to spend the following weekend at his estate, which was named after one of Huysmans's books, I can't remember which one now, maybe *À Rebours* or *Là-bas*, perhaps it was even called *L'Oblat*, my memory is failing me, I think it was called *Là-bas*, and that was the name of the wine as well, and after issuing this invitation Farewell fell silent although his blue eyes remained fixed on mine, and I was silent too and, unable to meet Farewell's penetrating gaze, I modestly lowered my eyes, like a wounded fledgling, and imagined that estate where the critic's path was indeed strewn with roses, where knowing how to read was valued, and where taste was more important than practical necessities and obligations, and then I looked up again and my seminarist's eyes met Farewell's falcon eyes and I said yes, several times, I said yes I would go, it would be an honor to spend the weekend at the estate of Chile's greatest literary critic. And when the appointed day arrived, my soul was a welter of confusion and uncertainty, I didn't know what clothes to wear, a cassock or layman's clothes: if I opted for layman's clothes, I didn't know which to choose, and if I opted for the cassock, I was worried about making the wrong impression. Nor did I know what books to take for the train journey there and back, perhaps a *History of Italy* for the outward journey, perhaps Farewell's *Anthology of Chilean Poetry* for the return journey. Or maybe the other way round. And I didn't know which writers (Farewell always invited writers to his estate) I might meet at Là-bas, perhaps the poet Uribarrena, author of splendid sonnets on religious themes, perhaps Montoya Eyzaguirre, a fine and concise prose stylist, perhaps Baldomero Lizamendi Errázuriz, the celebrated and orotund historian. All three were friends of Farewell. But given the number of Farewell's friends and enemies speculation was idle. When the appointed day arrived, my heart was heavy as I felt the train pull out of the station, but at the same time I was ready to swallow whatever bitter draughts God in his wisdom had prepared for me. I remember as clearly as if it were today (indeed more clearly still) the Chilean countryside and the Chilean cows with their black splotches (or white ones, depending) grazing beside the railway lines. From time to time the clickety-clack of the train set me dozing. I shut my eyes. I shut them as I am shutting them now. But then I opened them again suddenly, and there before me was the landscape: varied, rich, exultant and melancholy by turns. When the train arrived in Chillán, I took a taxi which dropped me in a village called Querquén, in what I suppose was the main square, although it was not much of a square and showed no signs of human presence. I paid the taxi driver, got out with my suitcase, surveyed my surroundings, and just as I was turning to ask the driver something or get back into the taxi and return forthwith to Chillán and then to Santiago, it sped off without warning, as if the somewhat ominous solitude of the place had unleashed atavistic fears in the driver's mind. For a moment I too was afraid. I must have been a sorry sight standing there helplessly with my suitcase from the seminary, holding a copy of Farewell's *Anthology* in one hand. Some birds flew out from behind a clump of trees. They seemed to be screaming the name of that forsaken village, Querquén, but they also seemed to be enquiring who: *quién, quién, quién.* I said a hasty prayer and headed for a wooden bench, there to recover a composure more in keeping with what I was, or what at the time I considered myself to be. Our Lady, do not abandon your servant, I murmured, while the black birds, about twenty-five centimeters in length, cried *quién, quién, quién,* Our Lady of Lourdes, do not abandon your poor priest, I murmured, while other birds, about ten centimeters long, brown in color, or brownish, rather, with white breasts, called out, but not as loudly, *quién, quién, quién.* Our Lady of Suffering, Our Lady of Insight, Our Lady of Poetry, do not leave your devoted subject at the mercy of the elements, I murmured, while several tiny birds, magenta, black, fuchsia, yellow and blue in color, wailed *quién, quién, quién,* at which point a cold wind sprang up suddenly, chilling me to the bone. Then, at the end of the dirt road, there appeared a sort of tilbury or cabriolet or carriage pulled by two horses, one cream, one piebald, and, as it drew near, its silhouette looming on the horizon cut a figure I can only describe as ruinous, as if that equipage were coming to take someone away to Hell. When it was only a few meters from me, the driver, a farmer wearing just a smock and a sleeveless vest in spite of the cold, asked me if I was Mr. Urrutia Lacroix. He mangled not only my second name, but the first as well. I said yes, I was the man he was looking for. Then, without a word, the farmer climbed down, put my suitcase in the back of the carriage and invited me to take a seat beside him. Suspicious, and numbed by the icy wind coming down off the slopes of the Cordillera, I asked him if he was from Mr. Farewell's estate. No I'm not, said the farmer. You're not from Là-bas? I asked through chattering teeth. Yes I am, but I don't know any Mr. Farewell, replied the good soul. Then I understood what should have been obvious from the start. Farewell was the critic's pseudonym. I tried to remember his real name. I knew that his first family name was González, but I could not remember the second, and for a few moments I was in two minds as to whether I should say I was a guest of Mr. González, plain Mr. González, or keep quiet. I decided to keep quiet. I leaned back against the seat and shut my eyes. The farmer asked if I was feeling ill. I heard his voice, faint as a whisper, snatched away immediately by the wind, and just then I remembered Farewell's second family name: Lamarca. I am a guest of Mr. González Lamarca, I said, heaving a sigh of relief. He is expecting you, said the farmer. As we left Querquén and its birds behind I felt a sense of triumph. Farewell was waiting for me at Là-bas with a young poet whose name was unfamiliar to me. They were both in the living room, although the expression "living room" is woefully inadequate to describe that combination of library and hunting lodge, lined with shelves full of encyclopedias, dictionaries and souvenirs that Farewell had bought on his journeys through Europe and North Africa, as well as at least a dozen mounted heads, including those of a pair of pumas bagged by Farewell's father, no less. They were talking about poetry, naturally, and although they broke off their conversation when I arrived, as soon as I had been shown to my room on the second floor, they took it up again. I remember that although I wanted to participate, as indeed they kindly invited me to do, I chose to remain silent. As well as being interested in criticism, I also wrote poetry and my intuition told me that to immerse myself in the lively and effervescent conversation Farewell was having with the young poet would be like putting to sea in stormy waters. I remember we drank cognac and at one point, while I was looking over the hefty tomes of Farewell's library, I felt deeply disconsolate. Every now and then, Farewell burst into excessively sonorous laughter. At each of these guffaws, I looked at him out of the corner of my eye. He looked like the god Pan, or Bacchus in his den, or some demented Spanish conquistador ensconced in a southern fort. The young bard's laugh, by contrast, was slender as wire, nervous wire, and always followed Farewell's guffaw, like a dragonfly following a snake. At some point Farewell announced that he was expecting other guests for dinner that night. I turned my head and pricked up my ears, but our host was giving nothing away. Later I went out for a stroll in the gardens of the estate. I must have lost my way. I felt cold. Beyond the gardens lay the country, wilderness, the shadows of the trees that seemed to be calling me. It was unbearably damp. I came across a cabin or maybe it was a shed with a light shining in one of its windows. I went up to it. I heard a man laughing and a woman protesting. The door of the cabin was ajar. I heard a dog barking. I knocked and went in without waiting for a reply. There were three men sitting around a table, three of Farewell's farmhands, and, beside a wood stove, two women, one old, the other young, who, as soon as they saw me, came and took my hands in theirs. Their hands were rough. How good of you to come, Father, said the older woman, kneeling before me and pressing my hand to her lips. I was afraid and disgusted, but I let her do it. The men had risen from their seats. Sit yourself down, son, I mean Father, said one of them. Only then did I realize with a shudder that I was still wearing the cassock I had traveled in. I could have sworn I had changed when I went up to the room Farewell had set aside for me. Yet although I had intended to change, I had not in fact done so, going back down to join Farewell in the hunting lodge dressed as before. And there in the farmers' shed I realized there would be no time to change before dinner. And I thought Farewell would form a false impression of me. And I thought the young poet he had in tow would also get the wrong idea. And finally I thought of the surprise guests, who were no doubt important people, and I saw myself wearing a cassock covered with dust from the road and soot from the train and pollen from the paths that lead to Là-bas, sitting cowed in a corner, away from the table, eating my dinner and not daring to look up. And then I heard one of the farmhands inviting me to take a seat. And like a sleepwalker I sat down. And I heard one of the women saying Father, won't you try some of this or that. And someone was talking to me about a sick child, but with such poor diction I couldn't tell if the child was sick or dead already. What did they need me for? If the child was dying, they should have called a doctor. If the child had already been dead for some time, they should have been saying novenas. They should have been tending his grave. Getting rid of some of that couch grass that was growing everywhere. They should have been remembering him in their prayers. I couldn't be everywhere at once, for God's sake. I simply couldn't. Is he baptized? I heard myself ask. Yes, Father. Good, all's in order then. Would you like a piece of bread, Father? I'll try it, I said. They put a chunk of bread in front of me. Hard bread, peasants' bread, baked in a clay oven. I lifted a slice to my lips. And then I thought I saw the wizened youth standing in the doorway. But it was just nerves. This was at the end of the fifties and he would only have been five years old, or six maybe, a stranger still to terror, abuse and persecution. Do you like the bread, Father? said one of the farmers. I moistened it with saliva. It's good, I said, very tasty, very flavorsome, a treat for the palate, veritable ambrosia, pride of our agriculture, hearty staple of our hardworking farm-folk, mmm, nice. And to tell the truth, the bread was not bad at all, and I needed to eat, I needed to put something into my stomach, so I thanked the farmers for their generosity, stood up, made the sign of the cross in the air, said God bless this house, and cleared out. Outside I heard the dog barking again and a rustle of branches, as if an animal hidden in the undergrowth were watching me make my uncertain way back towards Farewell's house, which I saw soon enough, lit up like an ocean liner in the southern night. When I arrived, the meal had not yet begun. Taking my courage in both hands, I re-solved not to change out of my cassock. I killed some time in the hunting lodge leafing through various early editions. On one wall the shelves were stacked with the finest and most distinguished works of Chilean poetry and narrative, each book inscribed to Farewell by the author with an ingenious, courteous, affectionate or conspiratorial phrase. It occurred to me that my host was, without doubt, the estuary in which all of our land's literary craft, from dinghies to freighters, from odoriferous fishing boats to extravagant battleships, had, for brief or extensive periods, taken shelter. It was no accident that his house had appeared to me shortly before in the guise of an ocean liner! But in fact, I reflected, Farewell's house was a port. Then I heard a faint sound, as if someone were crawling over the terrace. My curiosity piqued, I opened the French doors and went out. The air was even colder than before, and there was no one on the terrace, but in the garden I could make out an oblong-shaped shadow like a coffin, heading towards a sort of pergola, a Greek folly built to Farewell's orders, next to a strange equestrian statue, about forty centimeters high, made of bronze, and perched on a porphyry pedestal in such a way that it seemed to be eternally emerging from the pergola. The moon stood out clearly against a cloudless sky. My cassock fluttered in the wind. Boldly I advanced towards the place where the shadowy figure had hidden. There he was, next to Farewell's equestrian fantasy. His back was turned. He was wearing a velvet jacket and a scarf and a narrow-brimmed hat tipped back on his head, and he was softly intoning words that can only have been meant for the moon. I froze in a posture like that of the statue, with my left foot off the ground. It was Neruda. I don't know what happened next. There was Neruda and there a few meters behind him was I, and, between us, the night, the moon, the equestrian statue, Chilean plants, Chilean wood, the obscure dignity of our land. I bet the wizened youth has no stories like this to tell. He didn't meet Neruda. He hasn't met any of our Republic's major writers in a setting as elemental as the one I have just described. What does it matter what happened before and after? There was Neruda reciting verses to the moon, addressing the minerals of the earth, and the stars, whose nature we can only know by intuition. There I was, shivering with cold in my cassock, which suddenly felt several sizes too big, like a cathedral in which I was living naked and open-eyed. There was Neruda murmuring words I could not quite understand, but whose essential nature spoke to me deeply from the very first moment. And there was I, tears in my eyes, a poor clergyman lost in the immensity of our land, thirstily drinking in the words of our most sublime poet. And I ask myself now, propped up on my elbow: Has the wizened youth ever had an experience like that? I ask myself seriously: Has he ever in all his days experienced anything like that? I have read his books. In secret and wearing gloves, but I've read them. And there is nothing in them to match that scene. There's aimless wandering, street fights, horrible deaths down back alleys, the obligatory doses of sex, obscenity and indecency, dusk in Japan, not in Chile of course, hell and chaos, hell and chaos, hell and chaos. Oh my poor memory. My poor reputation. Now for the dinner. I cannot remember it. Neruda and his wife. Farewell and the young poet. Myself. Questions. Why was I wearing a cassock? A smile from me. Fresh-faced. I didn't have time to change. Neruda recites a poem. He and Farewell recall a particularly knotty line from Góngora. Naturally the young poet turns out to be a Nerudian. Neruda recites another poem. The meal is exquisite. Chilean tomato salad, game birds with béarnaise sauce, baked conger eel brought in specially from the coast on Farewell's orders. Wine from the estate. Compliments. After dinner the talk going on into the small hours, Farewell and Neruda's wife playing records on a green gramophone that caught the poet's fancy. Tangos. An awful voice reeling off awful stories. Suddenly, perhaps as a result of having consumed liberal quantities of liquor, I felt sick. I remember I went out on to the terrace and looked for the moon, in which our poet had confided earlier that evening. I steadied myself against an enormous pot of geraniums and fought back the nausea. I heard paces behind me. I turned around. There was Farewell's Homeric silhouette, facing me, hands on hips. He asked if I felt ill. I said no, it was just a little dizzy spell, the fresh country air would soon set me right. Although he was standing in the shadows, I knew that Farewell had smiled. Faintly, the sound of tango chords and the melodic complaints of a honey-smooth voice. Farewell asked what impression Neruda had made on me. What can I say, I replied, he's the greatest. For a few moments we stood there in silence. Then Farewell took two steps forward and his face appeared before me, the face of an aging Greek god kept awake by the moon. I blushed intensely. Farewell's hand came to rest for a moment on my belt. He spoke to me of night in the work of the Italian poets, night in Jacopone da Todi. Night in the work of the Penitents. Have you read them? I stammered. I said that at the seminary I had read a little of Giacomino da Verona and Pietro da Bescapé, Bonvesin de la Riva as well. Then Farewell's hand squirmed like an earthworm cut in two by a mattock and detached itself from my belt, but the smile remained upon his face. What about Sordello? he said. Which Sordello? The troubadour, said Farewell, Sordel also known as Sordello. No, I said. Look at the moon, said Farewell. I took a quick look at it. Not like that, said Farewell. Turn around and look properly. I turned around. I could hear Farewell murmuring behind me: Sordello, which Sordello? The one who drank with Ricardo de San Bonifacio in Verona and with Ezzelino da Romano in Treviso, which Sordello? (and at this point Farewell's hand gripped my belt once again!), the one who rode with Raymond Berenger and Charles I of Anjou, Sordello, who was not afraid, who was not afraid, who was not afraid. And I remember thinking then that I was afraid, and yet I chose to go on looking at the moon. The cause of my trepidation was not Farewell's hand resting on my hip. It was not his hand, it was not the moonlit night or the moon, swifter than the wind sweeping down off the mountains, it was not the sound of the gramophone serving up one awful tango after another, it was not the voice of Neruda or his wife or his devoted disciple, but something else, so what in the name of Our Lady of Carmen was it, I asked myself as I stood there. Sordello, which Sordello? repeated Farewell's voice sarcastically behind me, Dante's Sordello, Pound's Sordello, the Sordello of the *Ensenhamens d'onor,* the Sordello of the *planh* on the death of Blacatz, and then Farewell's hand moved down from my hip towards my buttocks and a flurry of Provençal rogues blustered on to the terrace, making my black cassock flutter, and I thought: The second woe is past, and, behold, the third woe cometh quickly. And I thought: I stood upon the sand of the sea, and saw a beast rise up out of the sea. And I thought: And there came one of the seven angels which had the seven vials, and talked with me. And I thought: For her sins hath reached unto heaven, and God hath remembered her iniquities. And only then did I hear the voice of Neruda, who was behind Farewell just as Farewell was behind me. And our poet asked Farewell who this Sordello was we were talking about, and who was this Blacatz, and Farewell turned to face Neruda, and I turned around too but all I could see was Farewell's back burdened with the weight of two, or perhaps three, libraries, and then I heard his voice saying Sordello, which Sordello? and Neruda's voice saying, That's precisely what I want to find out, and Farewell's voice saying, Don't you know, Pablo? and Neruda's voice saying, Why do you think I'm asking, dickhead? and Farewell laughing and looking at me, a look of brazen complicity, as if to say to me, Be a poet by all means if that's what you want to do, but you must write criticism, and for goodness' sake read widely and deeply, widely and deeply, and Neruda's voice saying, Well are you going to tell me or not? and Farewell's voice quoting a few lines from *The Divine Comedy*, and Neruda's voice reciting other lines from *The Divine Comedy* that had nothing to do with Sordello, and what of Blacatz, an invitation to cannibalism, Blacatz's heart of which we all should eat, and then Neruda and Farewell hugged one another and recited some lines by Rubén Darío, while the young Nerudian and I declared that Neruda was our finest poet and Farewell our finest literary critic and pair after pair of toasts were proposed. Sordello, which Sordello? Sordel, Sordello, which Sordello? Light and refreshing, swift and inquisitive, this little refrain followed me wherever I went, throughout the weekend. The first night at Là-bas I slept like a cherub. The second night I stayed up late reading a *History of Italian Literature in the Thirteenth, Fourteenth and Fifteenth Centuries*. On Sunday morning a car arrived with more guests. Neruda, Farewell and even the young Nerudian knew them all, but they were strangers to me, so while the others were busy greeting them effusively, I slipped away with a book into a wood that flanked the lodge on the left-hand side. Near the far side of the wood, but within it still, was a sort of hillock from which one could survey Farewell's vineyards and his fallow land and his fields of wheat and barley. On a path winding through the fields I could make out two farmers wearing straw hats, who disappeared into some willows. Beyond the willows stood very tall trees that seemed to be drilling into the majestic, cloudless sky. And further off still rose the great mountains. I said the Lord's Prayer. I shut my eyes. What more could I have wanted? Well, perhaps the murmur of a stream. The pure song of water on stones. As I walked back through the wood "Sordel, Sordello, which Sordello?" was still ringing in my ears, but something within the wood itself darkened the mood of that sprightly refrain. I came out on the wrong side. Before me lay not the lodge but some rather godforsaken-looking orchards. I was not surprised to hear dogs barking, although I could not see them, and as I walked through the orchards, where, under the protective shade of avocado trees, there grew an assortment of fruits and vegetables worthy of Archimboldo, I saw a boy and a girl, who, naked like Adam and Eve, were tilling the same furrow. The boy looked at me: a string of snot hung from his nose down to his chest. I quickly averted my gaze but could not stem an overwhelming nausea. I felt myself falling into the void, an intestinal void, made of stomachs and entrails. When at last I managed to control the retching, the boy and the girl had disappeared. Then I came to a sort of chicken coop. Although the sun was still high in the sky, I saw all the chickens sleeping on their dirty roosts. I heard the dogs barking again and what sounded like a body of considerable size crashing through the branches. It must have been the wind, I thought. Further on, I came to a stable and a pigsty. I went around them. On the far side stood a great araucaria tree. What was such a majestic, beautiful tree doing in that place? It has been set here by the grace of God, I said to myself. I leaned against the araucaria and took a deep breath. And there I stayed a while, until I heard some voices far in the distance. I set off again, sure that the voices were those of Farewell, Neruda and their friends come to look for me. I crossed a ditch where a sluggish stream of muddy water flowed. I saw thistles and all sorts of weeds, and I saw stones disposed in an apparently haphazard fashion, which was nevertheless the result of a human design. Who placed those stones in such a way? I asked myself. I imagined a child wearing a striped woollen sweater, several sizes too big, thoughtfully making his way through the immense solitude that precedes nightfall in the country. I imagined a rat. I imagined a wild boar. I imagined a vulture lying dead in a gully where no human being had ever set foot. Nothing came to sully that sure sense of absolute solitude. Beyond the canal I saw freshly washed clothes hanging from lengths of twine strung from tree to tree, billowing in the wind and giving off an odor of cheap soap. I pushed my way through the sheets and shirts, and there before me, thirty meters away, I saw two women and three men standing bolt upright in an imperfect semicircle, with their hands covering their faces. Just standing there like that. It was hard to believe, but there they were. Covering their faces! And although they did not remain for long in that position, three of them soon started walking towards me, the vision (and everything it conjured up), in spite of its brevity, completely upset my mental and physical equilibrium, that blessed equilibrium granted to me minutes before by the contemplation of nature. I remember I stepped back. I got tangled up in a sheet. I flailed around with my hands and would have fallen backwards had it not been for one of the farmers, who grasped my wrist. I ventured a puzzled, grateful grimace. That is what my memory has retained. My timid half-smile, my timid teeth, my voice breaking the silence of the countryside, saying thank you. The two women asked if I was all right. How do you feel, son, I mean Father? they asked. I was astonished that they had recognized me, because these were not the two peasant women I had seen on the first day, and I had seen no others since. Nor was I wearing my cassock. But news travels quickly, and these women, who did not work at Là-bas but on a neighboring estate, knew of my presence, and it is even possible that they had come to Farewell's property in the hope of hearing mass, something that Farewell could have organized without great difficulty, since the estate had a chapel, but of course the idea had not crossed Farewell's mind, largely because the guest of honor happened to be Neruda, who prided himself on being an atheist (although I suspect he was not), and because the pretext for the weekend gathering was literary rather than religious, and on that point I was in complete agreement. Nevertheless the women had come on foot through paddocks, along rough paths, around ploughed fields, just to see me. And there I was. And they looked at me and I looked at them. And what did I see? Rings under their eyes. Parted lips. Shiny skin stretched over cheekbones. A patience that I feared was not Christian resignation. A patience native to some faraway place, or so it seemed. Not a Chilean patience, although those women were Chileans. A patience that had not evolved in our land or anywhere in America, and was not even European, Asian or African (although I know practically nothing about the cultures of the latter continents). A patience that seemed to have come from outer space. And that patience almost wore my own patience out. And their words and their murmuring spread out through the surrounding countryside, among the trees swaying in the wind, among the weeds swaying in the wind, among the fruits of the earth swaying in the wind. And with each passing moment I felt more impatient, since I was expected back at the lodge, and perhaps someone, Farewell or someone else, was wondering why I had been away so long. And the women just smiled, looked severe or feigned surprise, mystery giving way to illumination on their initially blank faces, their expressions tense with mute questions or opening in wordless exclamations, while the two men who had remained behind started to move away, not walking in a straight line, not setting off towards the mountains, but zigzagging, talking to one another, now and then pointing out imperceptible features of the landscape, as if they too were prompted by nature to observe particularities worthy of commentary. And the man who had come forward to meet me with the women, the one whose claw had fastened on to my wrist and held me up, stood still about four meters away from the women and myself, but turned his head and followed the other two men with his eyes as they walked away, as if what they were doing or seeing was suddenly a source of fascination for him, sharpening his gaze so as not to miss the slightest detail. I remember scrutinizing his face. I remember drinking his face down to the last drop trying to elucidate the character, the psychology of such an individual. And yet the only thing about him that has remained in my memory is his ugliness. He was ugly and his neck was extremely short. In fact they were all ugly. The women were ugly and their words were incoherent. The silent man was ugly and his stillness was incoherent. The men who were walking away were ugly and their zigzag paths were incoherent. God have mercy on me and on them. Lost souls in the desert. I turned my back on them and walked away. I smiled at them, said something, asked them the way to the lodge at Là-bas and walked away. One of the women wanted to come with me. I refused. The woman insisted, I will escort you there, Father, she said, and the verb "to escort" sounded so incongruous in her mouth, it sent a wave of hilarity all through my body. You will escort me, will you? I asked. That I will, Father, she said. Or something like that, something a wind from the end of the fifties is still blowing around the innumerable nooks and crannies of a memory that is not mine. In any case I shuddered and shook with suppressed laughter. That won't be necessary, I said. You have been too kind already, I said. That will be all for today, I said. And I turned my back on them and walked away at a decidedly brisk pace, swinging my arms and wearing a smile that relaxed into unbridled laughter as soon as I passed through the barrier of washing, my walk at that point becoming a trot with a vaguely military rhythm to it. In the garden at Là-bas, beside a pergola built of fine timber, Farewell's guests were listening to Neruda recite. I approached quietly and stood beside his young disciple, who was smoking with a rather unpleasant frown of concentration on his face, while the words of the great man burrowed down through the various layers of the earth's crust and rose up to the pergola's carved crossbeams and beyond, to the Baudelairean clouds on their solitary voyages through the clear skies of Chile. At six that evening my first visit to Là-bas came to an end. A car belonging to one of Farewell's guests dropped me at Chillán, just in time to catch the train, which took me back to Santiago. My literary baptism had reached its conclusion. During the nights that followed, so many varied and often contradictory images crowded in on me, inhabiting my thoughts and my sleeplessness! Again and again I would see Farewell's black, rotund silhouette in an enormous doorway. His hands were in his pockets and he seemed to be intently watching time go by. I also saw Farewell sitting in a chair at his club, with his legs crossed, speaking of literary immortality. Ah, literary immortality. At times I could make out a group of figures joined at the waist, as if they were dancing the conga, up and down, back and forth in a salon whose walls were crammed with paintings. Somebody I could not see was saying, Dance, Father. I can't, I replied, it is contrary to my vows. With one hand I was holding a little notebook in which, with the other, I was drafting a book review. The book was called *As Time Goes By*. As time goes by, as time goes by, the whipcrack of the years, the precipice of illusions, the ravine that swallows up all human endeavor except the struggle to survive. The syncopated serpent of the conga line kept moving steadily towards my corner, lifting first its left legs all at once, then the right ones, and then I spotted Farewell among the dancers, Farewell with his hands on the hips of a woman who moved in the most exclusive circles of Chilean society at the time, a woman with a Basque surname, which unfortunately I have forgotten, while Farewell's hips in turn were gripped by an old man whose body was perilously frail, more dead than alive, but who beamed a smile at all and sundry and seemed to be having as much fun as anyone in the conga line. Sometimes, images from my childhood and adolescence would come back to me: my father's shadow slipping away down the corridors of the house as if it were a weasel, a ferret, or to employ a more appropriate simile, an eel in an inadequate container. All conversation, all dialogue, is forbidden, said a voice. Sometimes I wondered about the nature of that voice. Was it the voice of an angel? Was it the voice of my guardian angel? Was it the voice of a demon? It did not take me long to discover that it was my own voice, the voice of my superego guiding my dream like a pilot with nerves of steel, it was the super-I driving a refrigerated truck down the middle of a road engulfed in flames, while the id groaned and rambled on in a vaguely Mycenaean jargon. My ego, of course, was sleeping. Sleeping and toiling. It was around this time that I started working at the Catholic University. It was around this time that I published my first poems, my first reviews and my notes on literary life in Santiago. I prop myself up on one elbow, stretch my neck and I remember. Enrique Lihn, the most brilliant poet of his generation, Giacone, Uribe Arce, Jorge Teillier, Efraín Barquero, Delia Domínguez, Carlos de Rokha, all the gilded youth. All of them or almost all under the influence of Neruda, except for a few who succumbed to the influence or rather the teaching of Nicanor Parra. And I remember Rosamel del Valle. I knew him, of course. I reviewed them all: Rosamel, Díaz Casanueva, Braulio Arenas and his associates at La Mandrágora, Teillier and the young poets from the rainy south, the novelists of the fifties, Donoso, Edwards, Lafourcade. All of them good people, all of them splendid writers. Gonzalo Rojas, Anguita. I reviewed Manuel Rojas and wrote about Juan Emar, María Luisa Bombal and Marta Brunet. I published studies and explications of the work of Blest Gana, Augusto D'Halmar and Salvador Reyes. And I decided, or perhaps I had already decided, probably I had, it is all so vague and mixed up now, in any case I felt I needed a pseudonym for the critical articles, so that I could retain my real name for my poetical efforts. So I adopted the name of H. Ibacache. And little by little the reputation of H. Ibacache outstripped that of Sebastián Urrutia Lacroix, to my surprise, and to my satisfaction, since Urrutia Lacroix was preparing a body of poetic work for posterity, an oeuvre of canonical ambition, which would take shape gradually as the years went by, in a meter that nobody was using in Chile any more, what am I saying, a meter that nobody had ever used in Chile, while Ibacache read other people's books and explained them to the public, just as Farewell had done before him, endeavoring to elucidate our literature, a reasonable endeavor, a civilized endeavor, an endeavor pursued in a measured, conciliatory tone, like a humble lighthouse on the fatal shore. And Ibacache's purity—clothed as it was in the simple garments of critical prose, yet none the less admirable, since it was perfectly clear, whether reading between the lines or viewing the full sweep of the enterprise, that Ibacache was engaged in an ongoing exercise in dispassionate analysis and rationality, that is to say in civic virtue—Ibacache's purity would be able to illuminate far more powerfully than any other strategy the body of work taking shape verse by verse in the diamond-pure mind of his double: Urrutia Lacroix. And speaking of purity or while I'm on the subject of purity, one evening, when I was at the house of Don Salvador Reyes, with five or six other guests, Farewell among them, Don Salvador said that one of the purest men he had met in Europe was the German writer Ernst Jünger. And Farewell, who no doubt knew the story already, but wanted me to hear it from Don Salvador himself, asked him how and in what circumstances he had come to meet Jünger, and Don Salvador settled into an armchair with gilded trim and said that it had happened many years before, during the Second World War, in Paris, when he was on a diplomatic posting at the Chilean embassy. And then he told us about a party, I don't remember if it was at the Chilean embassy, or the German or Italian one, and he spoke of a very beautiful woman who asked if he would like to be introduced to the well-known German writer. And Don Salvador, who at that time must have been less than fifty years old according to my estimate, that is to say considerably younger and more vigorous than I am now, said, Yes, I would be delighted, please do, Giovanna, and the Italian woman, the Italian duchess or countess who was so fond of our eminent writer and diplomat, led him through various salons, each opening on to the next like mystical roses, and in the last salon there was a group of officers of the Wehrmacht and several civilians and the center of attention for all present was Captain Jünger, the First World War hero, author of *Storm of Steel, African Games, On the Marble Cliffs* and *Heliopolis*, and after listening to several of the great German writer's aphorisms, the Italian princess proceeded to introduce him to the Chilean diplomat, whereupon they exchanged views, in French naturally, and then Jünger, moved by a generous impulse, asked our writer if any of his works were available in French translation, to which the Chilean replied in a trice and the affirmative, yes indeed, a book of his had been translated into French, if Jünger would like to read it he would be delighted to present him with a copy, to which Jünger replied with a satisfied smile and they exchanged their cards and made a date to have dinner or lunch or breakfast together since Jünger's diary was crammed with inescapable engagements, not to mention the things that came up each day, inevitably upsetting the schedule of prior obligations, in any case they made a tentative date to meet for supper, a good Chilean supper, said Don Salvador, so Jünger could see for himself how well we live in Chile, in case he thought that over here we were still walking around wearing feathers, and then Don Salvador took his leave of Jünger and returned with the countess or the duchess or the princess through the series of salons opening one on to another like the mystical rose that opens its petals to reveal a mystical rose that opens its petals to reveal another mystical rose and so on until the end of time, speaking in Dante's Italian, speaking of Dante's women, but as far as the substance of the conversation was concerned they might just as well have been speaking of D'Annunzio and his whores. And some days later Don Salvador met Jünger in an attic room inhabited by a Guatemalan painter who had not been able to leave Paris since the beginning of the Occupation and whom Don Salvador visited from time to time, bringing on each occasion food of various kinds, bread and pate, a half bottle of Bordeaux, a kilo of spaghetti wrapped in brown paper, tea and sugar, rice and oil and cigarettes, whatever he could find in the kitchen at the embassy or on the black market, and this Guatemalan painter, subjected to our writer's charity, never thanked him, so even if Don Salvador appeared with a tin of caviar, plum marmalade and champagne, he never said, Thank you, Salvador, or Thank you, Don Salvador, and on one occasion, when visiting the painter, our eminent diplomat even brought with him one of his novels, a novel he had intended to give to someone else, whose name it were better discreetly not to mention here, since the person in question was married, and seeing the Guatemalan painter so down in the dumps, he decided to give him or lend him the novel, and when he came to visit the painter again, a month later, the novel, his novel, was still sitting on the same table or chair where he had left it, and when he asked the painter if he had disliked it or if on the contrary it had afforded him moments of pleasant diversion, the painter, withdrawn and ill at ease as he always seemed to be, replied that he had not read it, at which point Don Salvador, feeling downcast, as any author (at least any Chilean or Argentine author) would in such a situation, said: What you're telling me is you didn't like it; to which the Guatemalan replied that he neither liked nor disliked the book, he simply hadn't read it, and then Don Salvador picked up his book and on its cover he could see for himself the layer of dust that accumulates on books (indeed on all things) when they are not in use, and he knew then that the Guatemalan had told the truth, so he did not take offence, although at least two months passed before his next visit to the attic room. And when he returned the painter was thinner than ever, as if he had not eaten a thing during those two months, as if he were determined to let himself waste away while contemplating the street plan of Paris from his window, stricken with what in those days certain physicians described as melancholia, although we know it now as anorexia, a condition most common in young girls, like the Lolitas blown this way and that by the shimmering wind through the imaginary streets of Santiago, but which, in those years and in that city subjected to Germanic will, afflicted Guatemalan painters living in dim attic rooms at the top of precipitous stairs, and was not referred to as anorexia but melancholia, *morbus melancholicus*, the malady that beleaguers the pusillanimous, and then Don Salvador Reyes or perhaps Farewell, but if it was Farewell it must have been much later on, recalled Robert Burton's book, *The Anatomy of Melancholy*, which contains many perspicacious observations on that malady, and it may be that all those present at the time fell silent and held their peace for a minute in memory of those who had succumbed to the influence of black bile, the black bile that is eating away at me now, sapping my strength, bringing me to the brink of tears when I hear the wizened youth's words, and that night when we fell silent it was as if, in close collaboration with chance, we had composed a scene that might have figured in a silent film, a white screen, test tubes and retorts, and the film burning, burning, burning, and then Don Salvador spoke of Schelling (whom he had never read, according to Farewell), Schelling's notion of melancholy as yearning for the infinite—*Sehnsucht*—and cited neurosurgical operations in which the nerve fibers joining the thalamus to the cerebral cortex of the frontal lobe had been severed, and then he went back to the Guatemalan painter, skinny, wasted, rickety, pinched, scrawny, gaunt, haggard, debilitated, emaciated, feeble, drawn, in a word: extremely thin, so thin it frightened Don Salvador, who thought, This has gone on long enough, So-and-so (whatever the Central American was called), and like a good Chilean his first impulse was to invite the man out for dinner or supper, but the Guatemalan refused, on the pretext that for some reason or other he was incapable of going out into the street at that time of day or night, at which point our diplomat hit the roof or at least the table and asked him how long it had been since he had last eaten, and the Guatemalan said he had eaten a little while ago, just how long ago he didn't remember. Don Salvador however did remember a detail and that detail was this: when he stopped talking and put the few bits and pieces of food he had brought with him on the sideboard beside the gas burner, in other words, when silence reigned once more in the Guatemalan's attic room and Don Salvador's presence became less obtrusive, busy as he was setting out the food or looking for the hundredth time at the Guatemalan's canvases hanging on the walls, or sitting and thinking and smoking to pass the time with a will (and an impassibility) possessed only by those who have spent long years in the diplomatic corps or the Ministry of Foreign Affairs, the Guatemalan sat down on the other chair, deliberately placed beside the only window, and while Don Salvador let time slip away sitting in the chair at the back of the room, watching the shifting landscape of his own soul, the gaunt, melancholic Guatemalan let time slip away watching the repetitive and unpredictable landscape of Paris. And when our writer's eyes discovered the transparent line, the vanishing point upon which the Guatemalan's gaze was focused, or from which on the contrary it emanated, well, at that point a chill shiver ran through his soul, a sudden desire to shut his eyes, to stop looking at that being who was looking at the tremulous dusk over Paris, a desire to be gone or to embrace him, a desire (arising from a reasonable curiosity) to ask him what he could see and to seize it then and there, and at the same time a fear of hearing what cannot be heard, the essential words to which we are deaf and which in all probability cannot be pronounced. And it was there, in that attic room, by pure chance, that some time later, Salvador Reyes happened to meet Ernst Jünger, who had come to visit the Guatemalan, guided by his aesthetic flair and above all by his tireless curiosity. And as soon as Don Salvador crossed the threshold of the Central American's abode, he saw Jünger in his snug-fitting German officer's uniform intently examining a two-by-two-meter canvas, an oil painting that Don Salvador had seen innumerable times and which bore the curious title *Landscape: Mexico City an hour before dawn*, a painting undeniably influenced by surrealism (to which movement the Guatemalan had attached himself in a determined if not entirely successful manner, never enjoying the official blessing of Breton's acolytes), and in which an eccentric interpretation of certain Italian landscape painters could be detected, as well as a spontaneous attraction, not uncommon among extravagant and oversensitive Central Americans, to the French Symbolists, Redon and Moreau. The painting showed Mexico City seen from a hill or perhaps from the balcony of a tall building. Greens and grays predominated. Some suburbs looked like waves in the sea. Others looked like photographic negatives. There were no human figures, but, here and there, one could make out blurred skeletons that could have belonged to people or to animals.

When Jünger saw Don Salvador, his face betrayed just a hint of surprise and then an equally subtle hint of pleasure. Of course they greeted each other effusively and exchanged the customary questions. Then Jünger started talking about painting. Don Salvador asked about German art, with which he was unacquainted. It seemed that Jünger was only really interested in Dürer, so for a good while they talked about Dürer exclusively. Both men became more and more enthusiastic. Suddenly Don Salvador realized that since arriving he had not exchanged a single word with his host. He looked around, while inside him a little alarm rang louder and louder. When we asked what had set off the alarm, he said he was worried that the Guatemalan had been arrested by the French police or, worse still, the Gestapo. But the Guatemalan was there, sitting by the window, absorbed (although "absorbed" is not the word, in fact it could hardly be less appropriate) in the unwavering contemplation of Paris. Relieved, our diplomat cleverly changed the subject and asked Jünger what he thought of the silent Central American's work. Jünger said that the painter seemed to be suffering from acute anaemia and that, clearly, the best thing for him to do would be to eat something. At that point Don Salvador realized that he was still holding the packets of food he had brought for the Guatemalan, a little tea, a little sugar, a round loaf of bread and half a kilo of goat's cheese that none of his Chilean colleagues would eat, purloined from the embassy kitchen. Jünger looked at the food. Don Salvador blushed and proceeded to put it on the shelves while explaining to the Guatemalan that he had "brought him a few little things." The Guatemalan, as usual, neither thanked him nor turned around to see the little things in question. Don Salvador recalled that for a few seconds the situation seemed perfectly ridiculous. Jünger and himself standing there, not knowing what to say, and the Central American painter refusing to budge from the window, obstinately keeping his back turned. But Jünger knew how to respond to any situation, and compensating for his host's torpor, made Don Salvador feel at home, drawing up two chairs and offering him Turkish cigarettes, which it seemed he kept exclusively for friends or unforeseen situations, since he himself smoked none that evening. Far from the idle but agitated and often indiscreet chatter of the Parisian salons, the Chilean writer and the German writer enjoyed a free-ranging conversation, touching on the human and the divine, war and peace, Italian painting and Nordic painting, the source of evil and the effects of evil that sometimes seem to be triggered by chance, the flora and fauna of Chile, which Jünger seemed to have read about in the works of his fellow countryman Philippi, who was at once a true Chilean and a true German, all the while drinking cups of tea prepared by Don Salvador himself (which the Guatemalan, when invited to join them, refused almost inaudibly), the tea being followed by two glasses of cognac from the supply that Jünger carried in his silver hip flask, and this time the Guatemalan did not say no, which made both writers smile discreetly at first, then laugh long and loud, proffering the appropriate witticisms. And then, when the Guatemalan had gone back to the window with his due ration of cognac, Jünger, returning to the canvas that had intrigued him, asked the painter if he had spent long in the Aztec capital and what impression his time there had left, to which the Guatemalan replied that the week or slightly less he had spent in Mexico City had left no more than a vague blur in his memory, and, in any case, he had painted that picture, now the object of the German's attention or curiosity, many years later, in Paris, without really thinking about Mexico at all, although under the influence of what, for want of a better expression, he called a Mexican mood. And that set Jünger musing on the sealed wells of memory, perhaps imagining that during his brief stay in Mexico City the Guatemalan had unwittingly stored away a vision that would not surface again until many years later, although Don Salvador, who was agreeing with everything the Teuton hero said, thought to himself perhaps it was not a question of sealed wells suddenly reopened, or in any case not the sealed wells Jünger had in mind, and as soon as this thought occurred to him his head began to buzz, as if hundreds of sand flies or horseflies were escaping from it, flies visible only through the prism of a hot, dizzy feeling, in spite of the fact that the Guatemalan's attic room could hardly have been described as a warm place, and the sand flies flew back and forth in front of his eyelids, transparently, like winged droplets of sweat, making the buzzing noise that horseflies make, or the noise that sand flies make, which is more or less the same, although of course there are no sand flies in Paris, and then Don Salvador, as he nodded in agreement once again, by this stage understanding only snatches of Jünger's oblivious disquisition in French, glimpsed or thought he glimpsed a part of the truth, and in that tiny part of the truth he could see the Guatemalan in Paris, the war already underway or about to begin, the Guatemalan already accustomed to spending long, dead (or dying) hours in front of his only window, contemplating the landscape of Paris, and *Landscape: Mexico City an hour before dawn* emerging from that contemplation, from a Guatemalan's sleepless contemplation of Paris, and in its own way the painting was an altar for human sacrifice, and in its own way the painting was an expression of supreme boredom, and in its own way the painting was an acknowledgement of defeat, not the defeat of Paris or the defeat of European culture bravely determined to burn itself down, not the political defeat of certain ideals that the painter tepidly espoused, but his personal defeat, the defeat of an obscure, poor Guatemalan, who had come to the City of Light determined to make his name in its artistic circles, and the way in which the Guatemalan accepted his defeat, with a clear-sightedness reaching far beyond the realm of the particular and the anecdotal, made the hair on our diplomat's arms stand up, or, in vulgar parlance, gave him goose bumps. And then, in a single draught, Don Salvador drained what was left of his cognac and started listening to Jünger again, who all this time had been holding forth imperturbably, while he, that is to say our writer, had become entangled in a spiderweb of futile thoughts, and the Guatemalan, predictably, remained slumped beside the window, his life seeping away in the obsessive and sterile contemplation of Paris. And having grasped the drift of the monologue without too much difficulty (or so he thought), Don Salvador was able to insert a word edgeways into that parade of ideas, which would have intimidated the great Pablo himself, if not for the modest tone, the unpretentious manner in which the German set out his creed in matters relating to the fine arts. And then the officer of the Wehrmacht and the Chilean diplomat left the attic room together, and as they went down the interminable, precipitous stairs to the street, Jünger said he did not think the Guatemalan would live until the following winter, an odd remark for him to make, since by then it was obvious to everyone that many thousands of people were not going to live until the following winter, most of them much healthier than the Guatemalan, most of them happier, most of them unmistakably endowed with a stronger will to live, but Jünger made the remark all the same, perhaps without thinking, or not wishing to confuse separate issues, and Don Salvador agreed once again, although, having known and visited the painter over a longer period, he was not so sure the Guatemalan would die, nevertheless he agreed: Of course, Quite so, or perhaps he just made that diplomatic hmm hmm noise that can mean absolutely anything. And a little while later Ernst Jünger went to dine at the house of Salvador Reyes, and this time the cognac was served in proper cognac glasses and they discussed literature sitting in comfortable armchairs and the meal was, well, it was balanced, as meals in Paris ought to be, in gastronomic as well as intellectual terms, and when the German was leaving, Don Salvador gave him one of his books translated into French, perhaps the only one, I don't know, according to the wizened youth no one in Paris has even the vaguest memory of Don Salvador Reyes, he's probably saying that to annoy me, it might be true that no one remembers Salvador Reyes in Paris, indeed even in Chile few people remember him and fewer still read his books, but that is not the point, the point is that when the German went home that night, in one of his suit pockets there was a book by Salvador Reyes, and there can be no doubt that he subsequently read the book, because he mentions it, in quite positive terms, in his memoirs. And that is all Salvador Reyes told us about his years in Paris during the Second World War. But one thing is certain and it is something to be proud of: in his entire memoirs, Jünger mentions only one Chilean, and that is Salvador Reyes. Not a single Chilean to be found, even darting timidly across the background of the German's writings, except for Don Salvador

Reyes. Not a single Chilean exists, as a human being or as the author of a book, in the dark, rich years of Jünger's chronicle, except for Don Salvador Reyes. And that night as I returned from the house of our storyteller and diplomat, walking with Farewell's dissolute shadow down a street lined with lime trees, I had a vision of torrential grace, burnished like the dreams of heroes, and, being young and impulsive, I told Farewell about it straightaway, but he was only interested in finding the quickest way to a restaurant whose cook had been highly recommended to him, I told Farewell that for an instant, as we were walking down that quiet street lined with lime trees, I had seen myself writing a poem in praise of a writer or his golden shadow asleep inside a spaceship, like a young bird in a nest of smoking, twisted iron wreckage, and the writer who had set out for immortality was Jünger, and the spaceship had crashed in the Andes, and the immaculate body of the hero among the wreckage would be preserved by the everlasting snows, while the writings of the heroes together with the scribes who serve those writings would compose a hymn to the glory of God and civilization. And Farewell, who was getting hungrier by the minute and walking as fast as his bulk would allow, looked at me over his shoulder as if he were thinking, What a windbag, and graced me with a mocking smile. And he said that Don Salvador's words seemed to have made quite an impression on me. Not a good thing. It's good to love. It's bad to be impressionable. All the while Farewell kept on walking. And then he said that the literature of heroism was vast. So vast that two people with diametrically opposed tastes and ideas could dip into it at random without any likelihood of hitting on the same thing. And then he fell silent, as if the effort of walking were killing him, and after a while he said: Jeepers I'm hungry, an expression I had never heard him use before and never heard him use again, and then he didn't say a word until we were seated in a rather squalid restaurant, where, as he proceeded to wolf down a rich and varied Chilean repast, he told me the story of Heroes' Hill or Heldenberg, a hill situated somewhere in Central Europe, perhaps in Austria or Hungary. Naïvely I imagined that the story Farewell was about to tell would have something to do with Jünger or with what, in a fit of enthusiasm, I had been saying about Jünger and the spaceship wrecked in the Cordillera, and the heroes setting out for immortality armed only with their writings. But what Farewell told me was the story of a shoemaker, a subject of the Austro-Hungarian Emperor, a merchant who had made a fortune importing shoes from somewhere and selling them somewhere else and then manufacturing shoes in Vienna to sell to the elegant inhabitants of Vienna and Budapest and Prague, and also to the elegant inhabitants of Sofia and Belgrade and Zagreb and Bucharest. An entrepreneur who had started with nothing, or maybe a precarious family business, which he had set on a firm footing and gradually built up, making the brand famous, for this manufacturer's shoes were prized by all those who wore them both for their exquisite appearance and their remarkably comfortable feel, and that, after all, was the idea, to marry beauty and comfort, a brand of shoes, and boots (both high and ankle), even slippers and mules, that were extremely long-wearing and resistant, shoes that, in a word, you could be sure would never give out on you halfway from A to B, and you could also be sure, no small merit in a shoe, that they would not produce calluses or aggravate existing ones, and as those who have had occasion to visit a podiatrist know, this is no laughing matter, a brand of shoes, in short, that stood as a guarantee of elegance and comfort. And among the clients of the shoemaker in question, the shoemaker of Vienna, was the Austro-Hungarian Emperor himself, and the shoemaker was invited or managed to get himself invited to receptions, at some of which the Emperor was present, along with his ministers and the field marshals or generals of the Imperial army, a number of whom were bound to arrive wearing riding boots or shoes from the workshops of the shoemaker, with whom they deigned to exchange a few words, a few insignificant but always polite phrases, reserved and discreet, tinged with the gentle, almost imperceptible melancholy of autumn palaces, which, according to Farewell, was characteristically Austro-Hungarian, while the Russians, for example, endured a winter-palace melancholy, and the Spaniards, although here I feel he was stretching the analogy somewhat, were afflicted with the melancholy of summer palaces and raging fires, and the shoemaker, encouraged, some say, by those marks of respect, or driven, according to others, by the needs of his disturbed psyche, began to cherish an idea that had germinated in his mind, and when, after careful cultivation, this idea was ready, he did not hesitate to propose it to the Emperor himself, although to gain an audience he had to mobilize every one of his military and political connections, as well as his acquaintances at the Imperial court. And when all the strings had been pulled, the doors began to open and the shoemaker crossed thresholds and passed through vestibules, entering rooms each darker and more magnificent than the one before, although it was a satin darkness, a regal darkness, in which footsteps did not echo, first because of the quality and thickness of the carpets, and secondly because of the quality and suppleness of the shoemaker's footwear, and when he was led into the final room, there, on an absolutely everyday chair, was the Emperor, accompanied by a number of his advisers, and although these advisers cast a cool and even perplexed gaze upon the shoemaker, as if they were thinking, What on earth is that individual doing here, what bee has got into his bonnet, what crazy plan has hatched in his mind and prompted him to request and obtain an audience with the sovereign of all Austro-Hungarians, the Emperor himself, by contrast, welcomed him with expressions of affection, as a father welcomes his son, and spoke of shoes and shoemakers, Lefebvre of Lyon, whose fine shoes were inferior to those of his dear friend, Duncan & Segal of London, whose excellent shoes were inferior to those of his loyal subject, and Niederle, based in a small German village whose name the Emperor could not remember (Fürth, the shoemaker reminded him), whose shoes were extremely comfortable but nevertheless inferior to those of his enterprising compatriot, and then they spoke of the hunt and hunting boots and riding boots and various kinds of leather and ladies' shoes, at which point the Emperor firmly steered the conversation towards more wholesome topics, saying, Gentlemen, Gentlemen, a little restraint, as if he had not brought up the subject himself and his advisers were to blame, which imputation they and the shoemaker were only too glad to accept, apologizing profusely, until finally they got down to the real reason for the audience, and while each of those present helped himself to another cup of tea or coffee or refilled his glass with cognac, all eyes turned expectantly towards the shoemaker, who, taking a deep breath, intensely aware of the moment's gravity, and moving his hands as if caressing the whorled petals of an inexistent but imaginable, indeed a probable, flower, began to explain his idea to the sovereign. And the idea was Heldenberg or Heroes' Hill. In a valley known to the shoemaker, between one village and another, there rose a hill, a limestone hill, with oaks and larches growing on its slopes and all sorts of bushes on the higher, craggier parts, a green and black hill, although in spring it put on colors worthy of the most exuberant painter's palette, a hill that was a joy to behold from the valley floor and a sight to meditate upon when viewed from the high ground on either side of the valley, a hill that seemed to have been transported from another world and set down there as a reminder to man, to steady the heart, to soothe the soul, to delight the senses. Unfortunately the hill had an owner, the Count of H., a large landholder in the region, but the shoemaker had already solved that problem by negotiating with the count, who had initially been unwilling to sell even an unproductive piece of his land, it went against his proprietary instincts, explained the shoemaker with a modest smile, as if he could see it from the other man's point of view, but finally, after a considerable sum had been offered, the poor count came around to the idea. The shoemaker's plan was to buy the hill and convert it into a monument dedicated to the heroes of the Empire. Not just the heroes of the past and the heroes of the present, but also the heroes of the future. In other words the hill would serve both as a cemetery and as a museum. How would it serve as a museum? Well, each hero the Empire had produced would have his life-size statue erected on the hill, and there would even be statues of certain foreign heroes, but only in very special cases. How would it serve as a cemetery? Well, that was simple: it would be the burial place for the heroes of the Fatherland, as nominated by a committee of army officers, historians and lawyers, all of whose decisions would have to be approved by the Emperor. So the heroes of the past, whose skeletons, or ashes rather, were in all likelihood irrecoverably lost, would rest in peace forever on that hill, represented by statues, which would reflect as accurately as possible what was known about their physical characteristics from history or legends or oral traditions or novels, along with contemporary and future heroes, whose bodies could be got hold of, so to speak, by the civil servants of the Empire. What did the shoemaker ask of the Emperor? First of all, his consent and blessing, a sign that the project met with his approval, secondly, the financial support of the state, since on his own he could not meet all the costs involved in such a pharaonic enterprise. In short, the shoemaker was prepared to pay from his own pocket for the acquisition of Heroes' Hill, its conversion into a cemetery, the fence that would surround it, the paths that would give every visitor access to its furthest corners, and even the statues of certain heroes who were very dear to his patriotic heart, as well as providing for three gamekeepers already employed on one of his country properties, who could work as cemetery guards and gardeners, single, strong men one could rely on to dig a grave or drive away nocturnal tomb raiders. The rest, that is to say, the hiring of sculptors, the purchase of stone, marble and bronze, the ongoing administration, permits and publicity, shifting the statues, the road connecting Heroes' Hill to the main Vienna road, the ceremonies that would be have to be organized at the site, transport for families of the deceased and mourners, the construction of a small (or not so small) church, etc., etc., all this was to be paid for by the state. And then the shoemaker expatiated on the beneficial moral effects of such a monument and spoke of the old values, what remained when all else fled, the twilight of human endeavor, thought flickering before the onset of darkness, and when he had finished speaking, the Emperor, with tears in his eyes, took the shoemaker's hands, leaned close to his ear, and, in a voice that was choked with emotion yet firm, whispered words that nobody else could hear, then he looked into the shoemaker's eyes with a gaze it was not easy to meet, but the shoemaker, also on the brink of tears, met it without blinking, and then the Emperor nodded his head several times, reaffirming his assent, and looking at his advisers, said, Bravo, perfect, excellent, to which they replied, Bravo, bravo. So that was that, and the shoemaker left the palace rubbing his hands, beaming joyfully. Just a few days later the sale of Heroes' Hill was sealed, and the impetuous shoemaker, without waiting for an official confirmation, gave the go-ahead for a team of laborers to undertake the first stages of the project, supervising them personally, having found humble lodgings in the nearest hamlet or village, without a thought for his personal comfort, deeply absorbed in his work as only an artist can be, regardless of the weather, oblivious to the rain that often flooded the fields in that part of the country and the storms that traversed the steel-gray skies of Austria or Hungary, marching inexorably westwards, storms like hurricanes drawn towards the shadowy masses of the Alps, and the shoemaker watched them pass, water dripping from his overcoat and dripping from his trousers, his shoes sinking into the mud but not leaking at all, an absolutely magnificent pair of shoes, to which no praise or rather only the praise of a true artist could do justice, a pair of shoes for dancing or running or working in the mud, a pair of shoes that would never leave their owner in the lurch or let him down, and to which, sadly, the shoemaker paid scant attention (his assistant, having brushed off the mud, polished them every night, he or the young pot-boy at the inn, while the shoemaker lay exhausted, sprawled on the rumpled sheets, sometimes not even properly undressed), absorbed as he was in his obsessional dream, marching on through his nightmares, on the far side of which Heroes' Hill awaited him always, grave and quiet, dark and noble, his project, the work of which only fragments are known to us, the work we sometimes think we know but which in fact we hardly know at all, the mystery we carry in our hearts and which in a moment of rapture we set in the center of a metal tray inscribed with Mycenaean characters, characters that stammer out our history and our hopes, but what they stammer out in fact is nothing more than our defeat, the joust in which we have fallen although we do not know it, and we have set our heart in the middle of that cold tray, our heart, our heart, and the shoemaker shivered in his bed and went on repeating the word *heart* and also the word *gleam* and it seemed he was drowning and his assistant came into the room at that cold inn and spoke to him in comforting words, Wake up, Sir, it's only a dream, Sir, and when the shoemaker opened his eyes, eyes which a few seconds before had beheld his heart still beating in the middle of a tray, his assistant offered him a cup of warm milk, to which his only reply was a half-hearted swipe, as if the shoemaker were attempting to brush away his nightmares, and then, looking at his assistant as if he hardly recognized him, the shoemaker told him to stop fooling around with milk and bring him a glass of cognac or some eau-de-vie. And so he went on, day after day and night after night, in fair weather and foul, digging deep into his own funds, since the Emperor, after having wept and cried, Bravo, excellent, had not said another word, and his ministers too had opted for silence, likewise the most enthusiastic of the advisers, generals and colonels, and although without investors the project could not go ahead, the shoemaker had got it going all the same, and now it was too late to stop it. He was hardly to be seen in Vienna any more, and only when engaged in fruitless petitioning, for he spent every minute he could at Heroes' Hill, supervising the work of his ever less numerous laborers, mounted on a hardy hack or nag inured to the inclement weather, as tough and stubborn as its master, who, when the situation called for it, would not hesitate to dismount and get his hands dirty. At first, news of his idea spread like nimble wildfire lit by a mocking god to amuse the public, but then it went the way of all things, subsiding into oblivion. A day came when nobody mentioned his name any more. And then a day when people began to forget his face. His shoemaking business probably fared better than he did over the years. Occasionally someone, an old acquaintance, would see him in the streets of Vienna, but the shoemaker no longer greeted anyone or replied to greetings, and no one was surprised when he crossed to the other side of the street. A difficult, confusing period had begun, a terrible period indeed, in which difficulty, confusion and cruelty were as one. Writers went on invoking their muses. The Emperor died. A war broke out and the Empire collapsed. Composers went on composing and the public kept going to concerts. Nobody remembered the shoemaker any more, except, at odd and fleeting moments, the lucky few who still had a pair of his splendid, long-wearing shoes. For the shoemaking business too had been affected by the worldwide crisis and it changed hands and disappeared. The following years were even more confused and difficult. People were assassinated and persecuted. Then another war broke out, the most terrible war of all. And one day Soviet tanks rolled into the valley and, looking through binoculars from the turret of his armored vehicle, the colonel in charge of the tank regiment saw Heroes' Hill. And the caterpillar tracks creaked as the tanks approached the hill, which gleamed like dark metal in the last rays of the sun fanning out across the valley. And the Russian colonel got down from his tank and said, What the hell is that? And the Russians in the other tanks got out too and stretched their legs and lit cigarettes and stared at the fence of black wrought iron surrounding the hill and the massive gate and the letters cast in bronze, mounted on a rock at the entrance to inform the visitor that this was Heldenberg. And a farm laborer, who as a child had worked there, said when asked that it was a cemetery, the cemetery where all the heroes of the world would be buried. And then, after having broken open three big, rusty padlocks, the colonel and his men went in through the gate, and walked along the paths of Heroes' Hill. And they saw neither statues nor tombs but only desolation and neglect, until at the very top of the hill they discovered a crypt that looked like a safe, with a sealed door, which they proceeded to open. Inside the crypt, sitting on a grand stone seat, they found the shoemaker's body, his eye sockets empty as if he were never to contemplate anything but the valley spread out below Heroes' Hill, and his jaw hanging open, as if he were still laughing after having glimpsed immortality, said Farewell. And then he said: Do you understand? Do you understand? And once again I saw my father as the shadow of a weasel or a stoat scurrying from corner to corner in the house, and that house with its dim corners was like my vocation. And then Farewell repeated: Do you understand? Do you understand? while we ordered coffee and the people in the street rushed by, spurred on by an incomprehensible longing to get home, casting their shadows one after another, more and more quickly, on the walls of the restaurant where, undaunted by the agitation or perhaps I should say undaunted by the electromagnetic device that had been set off in the streets of Santiago and in the collective consciousness of the city's inhabitants, Farewell and I stayed put and kept still, only our hands moving, lifting the coffee cups to our lips, while our eyes looked on, as if what they were seeing had nothing to do with us, as if we hadn't noticed what was going on, in that typically Chilean way, watching the shadow play, figures appearing and disappearing like black flashes on the partition wall, a spectacle that seemed to have a hypnotic effect on Farewell while making me feel dizzy and causing an ache in my eyes that spread to my temples and then to the parietal bones and finally to the whole of my skull, an ache I soothed with prayers and aspirin, although, on that occasion, as I remember it now, struggling to prop myself up on one elbow, as if the moment of my heavenly flight were imminent, the pain persisted only in my eyes, and so could easily have been overcome, since shutting them would have disposed of the problem, and I could and should have done just that, but I did not, for there was something in Farewell's expression, something in his stillness, hardly disturbed by a slight eye movement, which, as I went on looking at him, seemed with growing force to imply an infinite terror, or rather a terror shooting towards the infinite, as terror does by its very nature, rising and rising endlessly, thence our affliction, thence our grief, thence certain interpretations of Dante, stemming from that terror, slender and defenceless as a worm, and yet able to climb and climb and expand like one of Einstein's equations, and Farewell's expression, as I was saying, seemed somehow to imply this, although, had anyone passed our table and looked at him, they would only have seen a respectable-looking gentleman in a rather pensive mood. And then Farewell opened his mouth, and I thought he was going to ask me once again if I had understood, but he said: Pablo's going to win the Nobel Prize. And he said it as if he were sobbing in the middle of an ashen field. And he said: America is going to change. And he said: Chile is going to change. And then his jawbone hung out of joint, but still he said: I won't live to see it. And I said: Farewell, you'll see it, you'll see it all. And then I knew that my words did not refer to heaven or eternal life, for I was pronouncing my first prophecy: if what Farewell had predicted was to happen, he would witness it. And Farewell said: The story of that Austrian has saddened me, Urrutia. And I: You have many years left to live, Farewell. And he: What's the use, what use are books, they're shadows, nothing but shadows. And I: Like the shadows you have been watching? And Farewell: Quite. And I: There's a very interesting book by Plato on precisely that subject. And Farewell: Don't be an idiot. And I: What are those shadows telling you, Farewell, what is it? And Farewell: They are telling me about the multiplicity of readings. And I: Multiple, perhaps, but thoroughly mediocre and miserable. And Farewell: I don't know what you're talking about. And I: The blind, Farewell, the stumbling of the blind, their futile flailing around, their bumping and tripping, their staggering and falling, their general debilitation. And Farewell: I don't know what you're talking about, what's happened to you, I've never seen you like this. And I: I'm glad to hear you say that. And Farewell: I don't know what I'm saying any more, I want to talk, but all that comes out is drivel. And I: Can you make out anything clearly in that shadow play? Can you see particular scenes, or the whirlpool of history, or a crazy ellipse? And Farewell: I can see a rural scene. And I: Something like a group of farmers praying, going away, coming back, praying and going away again? And Farewell: I see whores stopping for a fraction of a second to contemplate something important, then heading off again like meteorites. And I: Can you see anything there about Chile? Can you see the future of our land? And Farewell: That meal didn't agree with me. And I: Can you see our Palatine Anthology in that shadow play? Can you read any names? Or recognize any profiles? And Farewell: I see Neruda's profile and my own, but, no, I'm mistaken, it's just a tree, I see a tree, the multiple, monstrous silhouette of its dead leaves, like a sea drying up, it looks like a sketch of two profiles, but actually it's a tomb out in the open, cloven by an angel's sword or a giant's club. And I: What else? And Farewell: Whores coming and going, a river of tears. And I: Be more precise. And Farewell: That meal didn't agree with me. And I: How odd, it doesn't look like anything to me, just shadows, electric shadows, as if time had speeded up. And Farewell: There is no comfort in books. And I: And I can see the future clearly, and I can see you there, living to a ripe old age, loved and respected by all. And Farewell: Like Doctor Johnson? And I: Precisely, to a T, you've hit the nail right on the head. And Farewell: Like the Doctor Johnson of this godforsaken strip of earth. And I: God is everywhere, even in the most outlandish places. And Farewell: If I weren't so drunk and didn't have such a gut-ache I'd ask you to hear my confession right now. And I: It would be an honor. And Farewell: Or I'd drag you into the bathroom and screw you good and proper. And I: That's not you talking, it's the wine, it's the shadows upsetting you. And Farewell: No need to blush, we're all sodomites here in Chile. And I: Not just our pitiable compatriots but all men are sodomites, each of us harbors a sodomite in the architrave of his soul, and it is our duty to prevail over that unwelcome guest, to vanquish him, to bring him to his knees. And Farewell: Now you're talking like a cocksucker. And I: Never, I have never done that. And Farewell: I won't tell anyone, I promise. Not even at the seminary? And I: I studied and prayed, prayed and studied. And Farewell: I promise I won't tell anyone, I promise, I promise. And I: I read St. Augustine, I read St. Thomas, I studied the lives of all the popes. And Farewell: Do you still remember those holy lives? And I: Indelibly etched. And Farewell: Who was Pius II? And I: Pius II, also known as Enea Silvio Piccolomini, born in the vicinity of Siena, Supreme Pontiff from 1458 to 1464, attended the Council of Basel, secretary to Cardinal Capranica, spent time in the service of the Antipope Felix V, then in the service of the Emperor Frederic III, who crowned him poet laureate, he wrote verse you see, lectured at the University of Vienna on the classical poets, published a novel in 1444, *Euryalus and Lucretia*, in the manner of Boccaccio, just a year after publishing the said work, in 1445, he was ordained a priest and his life took a new turn, he did penance, admitted the error of his ways, became Bishop of Siena in 1449 and cardinal in 1456, obsessed with the idea of launching a new crusade, in 1458 he published the bull *Vocavit nos Pius*, in which he summoned the unenthusiastic sovereigns to the city of Mantua, in vain, later an agreement was reached and it was decided that a three-year crusade would be undertaken, but no one paid much attention to the Pope's grand words, until he let it be known that he was personally taking over command of the operation, Venice then forged an alliance with Hungary, Skanderbeg attacked the Turks, Stephen the Great was proclaimed *Atleta Cristi*, and thousands of men flocked to Rome from all over Europe, only the kings remained indifferent and unresponsive, so the Pope made a pilgrimage first to Assisi and then to Ancona, where the Venetian fleet was late to meet him, and when the Venetian warships finally arrived, the Pope was dying, and he said "Until this day I was wanting for a fleet, now the fleet must want for me," and then he died and the crusade died with him. And Farewell said: So he screwed up, like a typical writer. And I: He protected Pinturicchio. And Farewell: And who the hell was he? And I: A painter. And Farewell: I guessed that much, but who *was* he? And I: The one who painted the frescoes in the cathedral at Siena. And Farewell: Have you been to Italy? And I: Yes. And Farewell: Everything falls apart, time devours everything, beginning with Chileans. And I: Yes. And Farewell: Do you know the stories of other popes? And I: All of them. And Farewell: What about Hadrian II? And I: Pope from 867 to 872, there's an interesting story about him, when King Lothair II came to Italy, the Pope asked him if he had gone back to sleeping with Waldrada, who had been excommunicated by the previous pope Nicholas I, and then with trembling step Lothair approached the altar at Monte Cassino, which is where the meeting took place, and the Pope waited for him in front of the altar and the Pope was not trembling. And Farewell: He must have been a bit scared all the same. And I: Yes. And Farewell: And the story of Pope Lando? And I: Little is known about him, except that he was Pope from 913 to 914, and that he gave the bishopric of Ravenna to one of Theodora's protégés, who succeeded him on the papal throne. And Farewell: Funny name for a pope, Lando. And I: Yes. And Farewell: Look, the shadow play has finished. And I: Yes, you're right, so it has. And Farewell: How odd, I wonder what could have happened? And I: We'll probably never know. And Farewell: The shadows are gone, the rushing is gone, that feeling of being caught in a photographic negative is gone, was it just a dream? And I: We'll probably never know. And Farewell paid for the meal, and I accompanied him to his door, but did not want to go in, because everything was foundering, as the poet says, and then I was walking alone through the streets of Santiago, thinking of Alexander III and Urban IV and Boniface VIII, while a fresh breeze caressed my face, trying to wake me up properly, but still I cannot have been properly awake, for deep in my brain I could hear the voices of the popes, like the distant screeching of a flock of birds, a clear sign that part of my mind was still dreaming or obstinately refusing to emerge from the labyrinth of dreams, that parade ground where the wizened youth is hiding, along with the dead poets who were living then, and who now, against the certainty of imminent oblivion, are erecting a miserable crypt in my cranial vault, building it with their names, their silhouettes cut from black cardboard and the debris of their works, and although the wizened youth is not among them, since in those days he was just a kid from the south, the rainy borderlands, the banks of our nation's mightiest river, the fearsome Bío-Bío, all the same I sometimes confuse him with the swarm of Chilean poets whose works implacable time was demolishing even then, as I walked away from Farewell's house through the Santiago night, and continues to demolish now, as I prop myself up on one elbow, and will go on demolishing when I am gone, that is, when I shall exist no longer or only as a reputation, and my reputation resembling a sunset, as the reputations of others resemble a whale, a bare hill, a boat, a trail of smoke or a labyrinthine city, my reputation like a sunset will contemplate through half-closed eyelids time's little twitch and the devastation it wreaks, time that sweeps over the parade ground like a conjectural breeze, drowning writers in its whirlpools like figures in a painting by Delville, the writers whose books I reviewed, the writers whose work I criticized, the moribund of Chile and America whose voices called out my name, Father Ibacache, Father Ibacache, think of us as you walk away from Farewell's house with a dancer's sprightly gait, think of us as your steps lead you into the inexorable Santiago night, Father Ibacache, Father Ibacache, think of our ambitions and our hopes, think of our mute, inglorious lot as men and citizens, compatriots and writers, as you penetrate the phantasmagoric folds of time, time that we perceive in three dimensions only, although in fact it has four or maybe five, like the castellated shadow of Sordello, which Sordello? a shadow not even the sun can obliterate. Nonsense. I know. Twaddle. Piffle. Balderdash. Rot. Figments of the imagination that throng unbidden as one goes into the night of one's destiny. My destiny. My Sordello. The start of a brilliant career. But it wasn't always easy. Even prayer is boring in the long run. I wrote articles. I wrote poems. I discovered poets. I praised them. They would have sunk without a trace if not for me. I was probably the most liberal member of Opus Dei in the whole Republic. The wizened youth is watching from a yellow street corner and yelling at me. I can hear some of his words. He is saying I belong to Opus Dei. I have never hidden that, I say. But of course he's not even listening to me. I can see his jaws and his lips moving and I know he's shouting, but I cannot hear his words. He can see me whispering, propped up on one elbow, while my bed negotiates the meanders of my fever, but he cannot hear my words either. I would like to tell him this is getting us nowhere. I would like to tell him that even the poets of the Chilean Communist Party were dying for a kind word from me, a word of praise for their poetry. And I did praise their poetry. Let's be civilized, I whisper. But he cannot hear me. From time to time I catch a few of his words. Insults, of course. Queer, is he saying? Opus Dei? Opus Dei queer, did he say? Then my bed swings around and I can hear him no longer. How pleasant to hear nothing. How pleasant not to have to prop myself up on an elbow, on these poor old weary bones, to stretch out in the bed and rest and look at the gray sky and let the bed drift in the care of the saints, half closing my eyes, to remember nothing and only to hear my blood pulsing. But then my lips begin to work again and I go on speaking. I never pretended I wasn't a member of Opus Dei, young man, I say to the wizened youth, although I can no longer see him, although I no longer know if he is behind me or off to the side or lost in the mangrove swamps that line the river. I never made a secret of it. Everyone knew. Everyone in Chile knew. You must be the only person who didn't, or you're pretending to be more of a dimwit than you are. Silence. The wizened youth does not reply. In the distance I can hear what sounds like a gang of primates chattering away, all at once, in a state of high excitement, and then I take one hand out from under the blankets and put it in the water and laboriously steer the bed around, using my hand as an oar, moving my four fingers together like a punkah, and when the bed has turned around, all I can see is the jungle and the river and its tributaries and the sky, no longer gray but luminous blue, and two very small, very distant clouds scudding like children swept along by the wind. The chattering of the monkeys has died away. What a relief. What silence. What peace. A peace that summons the memory of other blue skies, other diminutive clouds scudding eastwards before the wind, and how they filled my spirit with boredom. Yellow streets and blue skies. As one approached the center of the city, the streets gradually lost that awful yellow color and turned into neat, gray, steely streets, although I knew that the slightest scratch would reveal yellow under the gray. And that filled my soul not only with lassitude but also with boredom, or maybe the lassitude began to turn into boredom, heaven knows, in any case there came a time of yellow streets and luminous blue skies and deep boredom, during which my poetic activity ceased, or rather my poetic activity underwent a dangerous mutation, since I did not actually stop putting pen to paper, but the poems were full of insults and blasphemy and worse, and I had the good sense to destroy them as soon as the sun came up the next day, without showing them to anyone, although at the time many would have considered it an honor to see them, poems whose deep meaning, or at least the meaning I thought I glimpsed in their depths, left me in a state of perplexity and anguish that lasted all day long. And this state of perplexity and anguish was accompanied by a state of boredom and exhaustion. Monumental boredom and exhaustion. The perplexity and the anguish were small by comparison, and lived encrusted in some cranny of the general state of boredom and exhaustion. Like a wound within a wound. And then I stopped giving classes. I stopped saying mass. I stopped reading the newspaper each morning and discussing the news with my brothers in Christ. My book reviews became muddled (although I did not stop writing them). Several poets came to see me and asked what was wrong. Several priests came to see me and asked what was troubling my spirit. I went to confession and prayed. But the rings under my eyes gave me away. And indeed at the time I was getting very little sleep, sometimes three hours, sometimes two. In the mornings I would walk from the rectory to the vacant lots, from the vacant lots to the shantytowns, from the shantytowns back to the center of Santiago. One afternoon two thugs attacked me. I swear I have no money, lads, I said to them. Don't you now, Father Ass'hole, replied the muggers. I ended up handing over my wallet and praying for them, but not much. My boredom had taken on a fierce intensity. And my exhaustion had grown in proportion. From that day on, however, I changed the route of my daily walk. I chose less dangerous parts of town, I chose parts of town from which I could contemplate the magnificence of the Cordillera, this was when it was still possible to see the Cordillera at any time of year, before it was hidden by a blanket of smog. I wandered and wandered and sometimes I caught a bus and went on wandering with my head against the window and sometimes I took a taxi and went on wandering through the abominable yellow and the abominable luminous blue of my boredom, from the city center to the rectory, from the rectory to Las Condes, from Las Condes to Providencia, from Providencia to Plaza Italia and the Parque Forestal and from there back to the center and back to the rectory, my cassock flapping in the wind, my cassock like a shadow, my black flag, my prim and proper music, clean, dark cloth, a well in which the sins of Chile sank without a trace. But all that flitting around was to no avail. The boredom did not abate, indeed sometimes in the middle of the day it became unbearable and filled my head with ludicrous ideas. Sometimes, trembling with cold, I would go to a soda fountain and order a Bilz. I would sit on a bar stool and gaze all misty-eyed at the droplets running down the surface of the bottle, while somewhere inside me, a bitter voice was preparing me for the unlikely spectacle of a droplet climbing *up* the glass, against the laws of nature, all the way up to the mouth of the bottle. Then I shut my eyes and prayed or tried to pray while my body was seized with shuddering, and children and adolescents ran back and forth across the Plaza de Armas, spurred on by the summer sun, and the sounds of stifled laughter coming from all directions composed an all too pertinent commentary on my defeat. Then I took a few sips of iced Bilz and resumed my wandering. It was around that time that I met Mr. Raef and, a little later, Mr. Etah. Both were employed by a certain foreign gentleman, whom I never had the pleasure of meeting, to run an import-export business. I think they had a clam-tinning plant and shipped the tinned clams to Germany and France. I first encountered Mr. Raef (or Mr. Raef first encountered me) in a yellow street. I was walking along half frozen to death when I heard someone calling my name. I turned around and saw him: a middle-aged man, of average height, neither skinny nor slim, with a nondescript face, just slightly more indigenous than European in its features, wearing a light-colored suit and a most elegant hat, waving to me in the middle of the yellow street, not too far away, while behind him the earth was reflected in sheet upon sheet of glass or plastic. I had never seen him before, but it was as if he had known me all his life. He said he had heard about me from Fr. García Errázuriz and Fr. Muñoz Laguía, whom I held in high esteem and whose favor I enjoyed, and those wise men, he said, had recommended me warmly and without reservations for a delicate mission in Europe, no doubt thinking that an extended trip to the old continent would be just the thing to restore some of the cheerfulness and energy I had lost and was visibly still losing, as from the sort of wound that, refusing to heal, eventually causes the spiritual if not the physical death of the afflicted person. At first I was puzzled and reluctant, since Mr. Raef's line of business could not have been further removed from my own, but in the end I got into his car and let him drive me to a restaurant in the Calle Banderas, a place that had seen better days, called My Office, where Mr. Raef, without giving anything away concerning his real reasons for tracking me down, spoke instead of people I knew, Farewell among others, and various poets of the younger generation whom I was seeing frequently at the time, just to let me know that he was keeping tabs on the circles I moved in, not only my ecclesiastical colleagues but also the writers with whom I felt an affinity and even my professional contacts, since he also mentioned the chief editor of the newspaper in which I published my column. Nevertheless it was obvious that he didn't know any of those people well. Then Mr. Raef exchanged some words with the owner of My Office and shortly afterwards we made a hurried exit for reasons that remain unclear to me, and arm in arm we walked through the neighboring streets until we came to another restaurant, much smaller and less gloomy, where Mr. Raef was welcomed almost as if he were the owner, and there we ate our fill, although it was very hot outside, hardly the ideal weather for the consumption of such a copious and varied repast. For coffee he insisted we go to the Haiti, a repulsive place that collects the scum of the city offices, the middle management, vice-this, assistant-that and deputy-the-other-thing, who consider it good form to drink standing up at the bar or in bunches scattered about the establishment's barnlike space, fronted, as I remember it, by two large glass windows, from the ceiling almost down to the floor, so that the clients standing inside, with a coffee cup in one hand and a battered ring binder or briefcase in the other, provide a spectacle for the passersby, who simply cannot resist looking in, albeit from the corner of an eye, at the mass of bodies crowded there in legendary discomfort. And I was dragged along to this sordid place, a man like me, with a name, indeed with two names, and a reputation to think of, and a certain number of enemies and a great many friends, and although I tried to protest, to refuse, Mr. Raef could be persuasive when he wished. And while I stood in a corner with my back to the wall, unable to take my eyes off the front windows, waiting for Mr. Raef to come back from the bar with two steaming coffees, the best in Santiago according to the plebs, I began to wonder just what kind of business the said gentleman was going to propose. He made his way back to me and we began to drink our coffee, standing up. I remember he talked. He talked and smiled, but I couldn't hear a thing he was saying because the voices of the assistant-deputy-whatnots were making such a racket, they were so thick in the air of the Haiti that not a cranny was left for even one more voice. I could have leaned forward, I could have put my ear to the lips of my interlocutor, as the rest of the clients were doing, but I preferred not to do so. I pretended to understand and let my gaze wander about that chairless space. A few men returned my gaze. In some of those countenances I felt I could read signs of an immense pain. Pigs suffer too, I said to myself. And immediately I regretted that thought. Pigs suffer, it is true, and their pain purifies and ennobles them. A lantern came alight inside my head or perhaps inside my piety: pigs too are a hymn to the glory of the Lord, or if not a hymn, for that is perhaps an exaggeration, a carol, a ballad, a round in celebration of all living things. I tried to eavesdrop on other conversations. It was impossible. I could only hear the odd word, that Chilean intonation, words that meant nothing yet conveyed the infinite vulgarity and hopelessness of my compatriots. Then Mr. Raef took me by the arm and before I knew what was happening I was out in the street again, walking beside him. I'm going to introduce you to my associate, Mr. Etah, he said. There was a buzzing in my ears. I felt as if I were hearing it for the first time. We were walking along a yellow street. There were not many people about, although, from time to time, a man in dark glasses or a woman wearing a headscarf would disappear into a doorway. The import-export office was on the fourth floor. The elevator was out of order. A little exercise won't do us any harm, it's good for the digestion, observed Mr. Raef. I followed him. There was nobody at the reception desk. The secretary has gone to lunch, said Mr. Raef. I stood there puffing and panting, saying nothing, while my Maecenas tapped on the frosted glass window of his associate's office with the second joint of his middle finger. A shrill voice cried, Come in. After you, said Mr. Raef. Mr. Etah was sitting behind a metal desk, and when he heard my name, he got up, came around and greeted me effusively. He was slim, with fair hair and pale skin, and his cheeks were ruddy, as if he rubbed lavender water into them at regular intervals. He did not smell of lavender, however. He offered us each a seat and after looking me up and down went back to his place behind the table. My name is Etah, he said, with an *h* at the end. Understood, I said. And you are Father Urrutia Lacroix. The very same, I said. Beside me, Mr. Raef was smiling and nodding without a word. Urrutia is a Basque name, isn't it? It is indeed, I said. Lacroix, of course, is French. Mr. Raef and I nodded in time. Do you know where the name Etah comes from? I have no idea, I said. Take a guess, he said. Albania? You're cold, he said. I have no idea, I said. Finland, he said. It's half Finnish, half Lithuanian. Quite, quite, said Mr. Raef. In times long gone there was a good deal of commerce between the Finns and the Lithuanians, for them the Baltic Sea was like a bridge, or a river, a stream crossed by innumerable black bridges, imagine that. I am, I said. And Mr. Etah smiled. You're imagining it, are you? Yes, I'm imagining it. Black bridges, oh yes, murmured Mr. Raef beside me. And streams of little Finns and Lithuanians going back and forth across them endlessly, said Mr. Etah. Day and night. By the light of the moon or the feeble light of torches. Plunged in darkness, guided by memory. Not feeling the cold that cuts to the bone up there near the Arctic Circle, feeling nothing, just alive and moving. Not even feeling alive: just moving, inured to the routine of crossing the Baltic in one direction or the other. A normal part of life. A normal part of life? I nodded once again. Mr. Raef took out a box of cigarettes. Mr. Etah explained that he had given up smoking for good about ten years before. I refused the cigarette that Mr. Raef offered me. I asked about the job they were proposing and what it would entail. It's not so much a job as a fellowship, said Mr. Etah. We're mainly an import-export firm, but we're branching out into other areas, said Mr. Raef. To be precise, at the moment we're working for the Archiepiscopal College. They have a problem, and we're looking for the ideal person to solve their problem, said Mr. Etah. They need someone to undertake a study, and it's our job to find the person who fits the bill. We meet a need, we look for solutions. And do I fit the bill, I asked? No one is better suited to the task than you, Father, said Mr. Etah. Perhaps you might explain just what this task consists of, I said. Mr. Raef looked at me in surprise. Before he could protest, I told him I would like to hear the proposal again, but this time from Mr. Etah. Mr. Etah needed no further prompting. The Archiepiscopal College wanted someone to write a report on the preservation of churches. Naturally no one in Chile knew anything about the subject. In Europe, on the other hand, a good deal of research had been undertaken, and in some quarters there was talk of definitive solutions putting a stop to the deterioration of God's houses on earth. My task would be to go and see, to visit the churches at the forefront of the battle against dilapidation, to evaluate the various methods, to write a report and come home. How long would it take? I could spend up to a year traveling around various European countries. If my work was not completed within a year, an extension of six months could be granted. I would receive my full salary each month, plus an allowance to cover travel and living expenses in Europe. I could stay in hotels or in the parish hospices scattered the length and breadth of the old continent. Need I say it was as if the job had been designed especially for me. I accepted. During the following days I had frequent meetings with Mr. Etah and Mr. Raef, who were taking care of all the paperwork for my trip to Europe. I wouldn't say I warmed to them, however. They were efficient, that was clear from the start, but they were also sadly lacking in tact. And they knew nothing about literature, except for a couple of Neruda's early poems, which they could recite from memory and often did. Still, they knew how to solve what to me seemed insuperable administrative problems and did whatever was required to smooth the way to my new destiny. As the day of my departure approached, I became more and more nervous. I spent a good while saying goodbye to my friends, who couldn't believe my luck. I made an arrangement with the newspaper whereby I would go on sending reviews and installments of my column back from Europe. One morning I said goodbye to my elderly mother and took the train to Valparaíso, where I embarked on the *Donizetti*, a ship that plied between Valparaíso and Genoa under the Italian flag. The voyage was slow and refreshing and enlivened by friendships that have lasted right up to the present, if only in the most colorless and polite form, namely the punctual exchange of Christmas greetings by post. The first port of call was Arica, where, from the deck, I took a photograph of our heroic headland, then El Callao, then Guayaquil (when we crossed the equator I had the pleasure of saying mass for all the passengers), then Buenaventura, where, as the ship lay at anchor among the stars, I recited José Asunción Silva's *Nocturno* by way of an homage to Colombian letters, and was warmly applauded, even by the Italian officers, who, in spite of their imperfect grasp of Spanish, were able to appreciate the profoundly musical strains of the bard who died by his own hand, then Panama, the wasplike waist of the Americas, then Cristóbal and Colón, the divided city, where some rascals tried unsuccessfully to rob me, then industrious Maracaibo, redolent of oil, and then we crossed the Atlantic Ocean, where, by popular demand, I celebrated another mass for all the passengers, many of whom wanted to confess their sins during three days of storms and heavy weather, and then we stopped in Lisbon, where I got off the boat and prayed in the first church in the port, and then the *Donizetti* put ashore in Malaga and Barcelona, and finally, one winter morning, we arrived in Genoa, where I said goodbye to my new friends, and said mass for a few of them in the ship's reading room, a room with oak floorboards and teak-paneled walls and a large crystal chandelier hanging from the ceiling and soft armchairs in which I had spent so many happy hours, absorbed in the works of the classic Greek authors and the classic Latin authors and my Chilean contemporaries, having at last regained my passion for reading, my literary instincts, completely cured, while the ship went on parting the waves, faring on through ocean twilight and bottomless Atlantic night, and, comfortably seated in that room with its fine wood, its smell of the sea and strong liquor, its smell of books and solitude, I went on happily reading well into the night, when no one ventured on to the decks of the *Donizetti*, except for sinful shadows who were careful not to interrupt me, careful not to disturb my reading, happiness, happiness, passion regained, genuine devotion, my prayers rising up and up through the clouds to the realm of pure music, to what for want of a better name we call the choir of the angels, a non-human space but undoubtedly the only imaginable space we humans can truly inhabit, an uninhabitable space but the only one worth inhabiting, a space in which we shall cease to be but the only space in which we can be what we truly are, and then I stepped on to dry land, on to Italian soil, and I said goodbye to the *Donizetti* and set off on the roads of Europe, determined to do a good job, lighthearted, full of confidence, resolution and faith. The first church I visited was the church of St. Mary of Perpetual Suffering in Pistoia. I was expecting to find an old parish priest, so I was more than a little surprised to be welcomed by a clergyman not even thirty years old. Fr. Pietro, as he was called, explained to me that Mr. Raef had written to inform him of my visit, and went on to say that in Pistoia the principal threat to the major examples of Romanesque and Gothic architecture was pollution caused not by humans but by animals, specifically pigeon shit, the numbers of pigeons in Pistoia, as in many other European cities and villages, having increased exponentially. A radical solution to this problem had been found, a weapon that was still undergoing tests, as he was to show me the following day. That night, I remember, I slept in a room that opened off the sacristy, and I kept waking up suddenly, not knowing if I was on the boat or still in Chile, and supposing I was in Chile, was it our family home or the dormitory at school or a friend's house, and although I sometimes realized I was in a room adjoining the sacristy of a European church, I didn't quite know which European country that room was in and what I was doing there. In the morning I was woken by a woman who worked for the parish. Her name was Antonia and she said: Father, Fr. Pietro is waiting for you, get up quickly or you'll incur his wrath. Her very words. So I performed my ablutions and put on my cassock and went out to the patio of the presbytery, and there was young Fr. Pietro, wearing a smarter cassock than mine, his left hand clad in a stout gauntlet of leather and metal, and in the air, in the square space of sky bounded by gold-colored walls, I noticed the shadow of a bird, and when Fr. Pietro saw me he said: Let's go up the bell tower, and without a word I followed in his footsteps and we climbed up to the bell tower's steeple, tackling that silent, strenuous ascent in tandem, and when we reached the steeple, Fr. Pietro whistled and waved his arms and the shadow came down from the sky to the bell tower and landed on the gauntlet protecting the Italian's left hand, and then there was no need to explain, for it was clear to me that the dark bird circling over the church of St. Mary of Perpetual Suffering was a falcon and Fr. Pietro had mastered the art of falconry, and that was the method they were using to rid the old church of pigeons, and then, looking down from the heights, I scanned the steps leading to the portico and the brick-paved square beside the magenta-colored church, and in all that space, as hard as I looked, I could not see a single pigeon. In the afternoon, Fr. Pietro, one of God's keen falconers, took me to another place in Pistoia where there were no ecclesiastical buildings or civil monuments or anything that needed to be defended against the ravages of time. We went in the parish van. The falcon traveled in a box. When we reached our destination, Fr. Pietro took the falcon out and flung it up into the sky. I saw it fly and swoop down on a pigeon and I saw the pigeon shudder as it flew. The window of a council flat opened and an old woman shouted something and shook her fist at us. Fr. Pietro laughed. Our cassocks flapped in the wind. When we got back he told me the falcon was called Turk. Then I took a train to Turin, where I visited Fr. Angelo, curate of St. Paul of Succor, who was also versed in the falconer's art. His falcon, called Othello, had struck terror into the heart of every pigeon in Turin, although, as Fr. Angelo confided in me, Othello was not the only falcon in the city, he had good reason to believe that in some unidentified suburb of Turin, probably in the south, there lived another falcon, which Othello had occasionally encountered during his aerial forays. Both birds of prey hunted pigeons, and, in principle, there was no reason for them to fear one another, but Fr. Angelo felt the day was not far off when the two falcons would clash. I stayed longer in Turin than in Pistoia. Then I took the night train to Strasbourg. There Fr. Joseph had a falcon called Xenophon, with plumage of deepest midnight blue, and sometimes when Fr. Joseph was saying mass the falcon would be perched on a gilded pipe at the top of the organ, and kneeling there in the church listening to the word of God, I could sometimes feel the falcon's gaze on the nape of my neck, his staring eyes, and it distracted me, and I thought of Bernanos and Mauriac, whom Fr. Joseph read and reread tirelessly, and I thought of Graham Greene, whom I was reading, though he was not, since the French only read the French, in spite of which we stayed up late one night talking about Graham Greene, without being able to resolve our disagreement. We also talked about Burson, priest and martyr in North Africa, whose life and ministry were the subject of a book by Vuillamin, which Fr. Joseph lent to me, and about l'Abbé Pierre, a funny little mendicant priest of whom Fr. Joseph seemed to approve on Sundays but not during the week. And then I left Strasbourg and went to Avignon, to the church of Our Mother of Noon, in the parish of Fr. Fabrice, whose falcon, called Ta Gueule, was known throughout the surrounding area for his voracity and ferocity, and my afternoons with Fr. Fabrice were unforgettable, Ta Gueule in full flight, scattering not just flocks of pigeons but also flocks of starlings, which in those long gone, happy days, were common in the countryside of Provence, where Sordel, Sordello, which Sordello? wandered once, and Ta Gueule flew off and disappeared among the low clouds, the clouds descending from the desecrated yet somehow still pure hills of Avignon, and while Fr. Fabrice and I conversed, Ta Gueule appeared again like a lightning bolt, or the abstract idea of a lightning bolt, and swooped on the huge flocks of starlings coming out of the west like swarms of flies, darkening the sky with their erratic fluttering, and after a few minutes the fluttering of the starlings was bloodied, scattered and bloodied, and afternoon on the outskirts of Avignon took on a deep red hue, like the color of sunsets seen from an airplane, or the color of dawns, when the passenger is woken gently by the engines whistling in his ears and lifts up the little blind and sees the horizon marked with a red line, like the planet's femoral artery, or the planet's aorta, gradually swelling, and I saw that swelling blood vessel in the sky over Avignon, the bloodstained flight of the starlings, Ta Gueule splashing color like an abstract expressionist painter, ah, the peace, the harmony of nature, nowhere as evident or as unequivocal as in Avignon, and then Fr. Fabrice whistled and we waited for an indefinable time, measured only by the beating of our hearts, until our quivering warrior came to rest upon his arm. And then I took the train and with a heavy heart left Avignon behind and traveled to Spain, and of course the first thing I did was to go to Pamplona, where the churches were maintained by other methods, which did not interest me, or were simply not maintained at all, but I owed my Opus Dei colleagues a visit, and they introduced me to the Opus publishers and the principals of the Opus schools and the Rector of the University, which is also run by Opus Dei, and all of them showed an interest in my work as literary critic, poet and teacher, and they invited me to publish a book with them, the Spanish are so generous, and punctilious too, for the very next day I signed a contract, and then they gave me a letter addressed to me and written by Mr. Raef, in which he asked How's Europe going, what's the weather like and the food and the sites of historical interest, a ridiculous letter but somehow it seemed to conceal another, invisible letter, more serious in content, and this hidden letter, although I couldn't tell what it said or even be sure it really existed, worried me deeply. And then, after much hugging and writing down addresses and friendly, protracted farewells, I left

Pamplona and went to Burgos, where I was to meet Fr. Antonio, a little old priest with a falcon called Rodrigo, who didn't hunt pigeons, partly because Fr. Antonio was now too old to accompany the raptor on his forays, and partly because, after an initial period of enthusiasm, the priest had begun to have doubts about using such an expeditious method to be rid of birds which, in spite of their shitting, were God's creatures too. By the time I arrived in Burgos, Rodrigo the falcon was eating only mincemeat or sausage meat and the offal that Fr. Antonio or his housekeeper bought at the market, liver, heart, scraps, and idleness had reduced him to a sorry state, similar to the state in which Fr. Antonio was languishing, his cheeks hollowed by doubt and untimely repentance, which is the worst kind, and when I arrived in Burgos, Fr. Antonio was lying on his bed, a poor priest's Spartan pallet, under a coarse woollen blanket, in a big room with stone walls, and the falcon was in a corner, shivering with cold, wearing his hood, without the slightest trace of the elegance I had observed in his Italian and French counterparts, a wretched falcon and a wretched priest, wasting away the pair of them, and Fr. Antonio saw me, and tried to lift himself up on one elbow, just as I was to do years later, aeons later, two or three minutes later, when the wizened youth appeared like a bolt from the blue, and I saw Fr. Antonio's elbow and his arm as skinny as a chicken's leg, and Fr. Antonio told me he had been thinking, I have been thinking, he said, maybe this business with the falcons is not such a good idea, it's true they protect churches from the corrosive and, in the long term, destructive effects of pigeon shit, but one mustn't forget that pigeons or doves are the earthly symbol of the Holy Spirit, are they not? And the Catholic church can do without the Father and the Son, but not the Holy Spirit, who is far more important than most lay people suspect, more important than the Son who died on the cross, more important than the Father who made the stars and the earth and all the universe, and then with the tips of my fingers I touched the forehead and temples of the Castilian priest and realized immediately that he was running a temperature of at least 104 degrees Fahrenheit, and I called his housekeeper and sent her to fetch a doctor, and while I was waiting for the doctor to arrive, for something to do I examined the falcon, who seemed to be freezing to death, perched on a lectern, with his hood on, and seeing him there like that I felt it was wrong, so after getting another blanket from the sacristy and wrapping it around Fr. Antonio, I found the gauntlet and took the falcon and went out on to the patio where I contemplated the cold, crystal-clear night, and I removed the falcon's hood and said to him: Fly, Rodrigo, and after I had said it twice more, Rodrigo took flight, and I saw him rise, regaining his confidence, and his wings seemed vast and they made a sound like metal blades, and a wind like a hurricane sprang up, and the falcon veered from his vertical course and my cassock flew up like a flag in the grip of uncontrollable rage, and I remember at that point I cried out again, Fly, Rodrigo, and then I heard a sound of crazy, multitudinous flight, and the folds of my cassock covered my eyes while the wind swept the church and its surroundings clean, and when I managed to remove my own hood, so to speak, I saw bundles of feathers on the ground, the small bloody bodies of several pigeons, which the falcon had deposited at my feet, or within a radius of no more than ten meters from where I stood, before disappearing, for that was the last I saw of Rodrigo, he disappeared into the sky over Burgos, where there are rumored to be other falcons who prey on small birds, and perhaps it was my fault, perhaps I should have stayed out on the patio calling him, maybe he would have come back, but a little bell was ringing insistently from the depths of the church, and when the sound finally registered in my consciousness, I realized it was the doctor and the housekeeper, so I left my post and went to open the door for them, and when I came back to the patio the falcon was gone. That night Fr. Antonio died, and I celebrated the last rites and took care of the practicalities until the next day, when another priest arrived. The new priest didn't notice Rodrigo's absence. The housekeeper may have, but she looked at me as if to say it didn't matter to her. Perhaps she thought I had set the falcon free after Fr. Antonio's death or perhaps she thought I had killed the falcon according to Fr. Antonio's instructions. In any case she said nothing. The next day I left Burgos and went to Madrid, where nothing was being done to prevent the deterioration of churches, but I had other business to attend to there. Then I took a train and traveled to Namur in Belgium, where Fr. Charles, curate of Our Lady of the Woods, had a falcon called Ronnie, and Fr. Charles and I became good friends, we would often go cycling together through the woods surrounding the town, each with a basket full of picnic provisions and, without fail, a bottle of wine, and one afternoon Fr. Charles even heard my confession on the bank of a small river that flowed into a big river, on the grass, surrounded by wildflowers and tall oak trees, but I did not mention Fr. Antonio or his falcon Rodrigo, whom I had lost on that crystal-clear, irrevocable night. And then I took the train and said goodbye to the splendid Fr. Charles and set out for Saint Quentin in France, where I was welcomed by Fr. Paul, at the church of St. Peter and St. Paul, a little jewel of Gothic architecture, and a funny thing happened one day when Fr. Paul and I and his falcon Fever had gone out intending to clear the sky of pigeons, but there were none, much to my host's chagrin, for he was young and proud of his bird, which was, in his opinion, the finest of all raptors, and the church of St. Peter and St. Paul was close to the main square and the town hall, from which there came a murmur of voices that seemed to be annoying Fr. Paul, so there we were, he and I and Fever, ready and waiting, when suddenly we saw a pigeon appear from behind the red-tiled roof of one of the buildings on the church square, and Fr. Paul released his falcon, who dealt swiftly and firmly with that bird, which had flown across from near the town hall and seemed to be heading for the main steeple of the delightful church of St. Peter and St. Paul, and the pigeon, struck by Fever, fell from the sky, and a murmur of surprise came from the main square of Saint Quentin, and Fr. Paul and I, rather than beating a hasty retreat, left the church and walked towards the main square, and there was the pigeon, a white dove, bleeding on to the paving stones, and a crowd of people standing around it, including the Mayor of Saint Quentin, and a good number of sportsmen, and only then did we realize that the pigeon killed by Fever was the mascot for an athletic competition, and the athletes were visibly displeased or perturbed, likewise the local society ladies, who had sponsored the race and proposed the idea of opening the proceedings by releasing a dove, and the local communists were displeased too, since they had supported the ladies' proposal, although for them that dove, now dead but flying free just a moment before, did not symbolize the peaceful sublimation of rivalry in sport, for them it was Picasso's dove, a bird with a double meaning, so, in a word, all the good folk of Saint Quentin were upset, all but the children, who were searching wide-eyed for Fever's shadow in the sky, and had gathered around Fr. Paul to ask pseudoscientific and pseudotechnical questions about his marvelous bird, and Fr. Paul, with a smile on his face, apologized to those present, and gestured as if to say, Sorry, anyone can make a mistake, and then he turned his attention to the young ones, whom he amused with answers that were always Christian in spirit if sometimes a little free with the facts. And then I went to Paris, where I spent about a month writing poetry, frequenting museums and libraries, visiting churches whose beauty brought tears to my eyes, now and then drafting a bit of my report on the preservation of buildings of national historical interest, with special emphasis on the use of falcons, sending my reviews and articles back to Chile, reading the books that arrived from Santiago, eating and walking around. From time to time, for no particular reason, Mr. Raef sent me a brief letter. Once a week I would go to the Chilean embassy to peruse our national newspapers and chat with my friend the cultural attaché, a very Chilean, very Christian, not overly cultivated fellow, who was teaching himself French by doing the crossword in *Le Figaro*. Then I traveled to Germany, toured Bavaria, went to Austria and Switzerland. After that I went back to Spain. I traveled around Andalusia. Didn't think much of it. I returned to Navarre. Splendid. I visited the land of the Galicians. I went to Asturias and the Basque country. I took a train bound for Italy. I went to Rome. I knelt before the Holy Father. I cried. I had disturbing dreams. I saw women tearing their clothes. I saw Fr. Antonio, the priest from Burgos, who, as he lay dying, opened one eye and said: It's wrong, my friend, it's wrong. I saw a flock of falcons, thousands of falcons flying high over the Atlantic ocean, headed for America. Sometimes the sun went black in my dreams. Sometimes a very fat German priest appeared and told me a joke. Father Lacroix, he said to me, I'm going to tell you a joke. One day the Pope is having a quiet conversation with a German theologian in one of the rooms of the Vatican. Suddenly two French archaeologists burst in, very agitated and nervous, and they tell the Holy Father they have just got back from Israel with some very good news and some rather bad news. The Pope beseeches them to come out with it, and not to leave him in suspense. Talking over each other, the Frenchmen say the good news is they have discovered the Holy Sepulchre. The Holy Sepulchre? says the Pope. The Holy Sepulchre. Not a shadow of a doubt. The Pope is moved to tears. What's the bad news? he asks, drying his eyes. Well, inside the Holy Sepulchre we found the body of Christ. The Pope passes out. The Frenchmen rush to his side and fan his face. The only one who's calm is the German theologian, and he says: Ah, so Jesus really existed? Sordel, Sordello, that Sordello, the master. One day I decided it was time to go back to Chile. I went by plane. My country was not in a healthy state. This is no time to dream, I said to myself, I must act on my principles. This is no time to go chasing rainbows, I said, I must be a patriot. In Chile things were not going well. For me, things had been going well, but not for my country. I am not a fanatical nationalist, but I do sincerely love the land of my birth. Chile, my Chile. What on earth has come over you? I would sometimes ask, leaning out of my open window, looking at the glow of Santiago in the distance. What have they done to you? Have my countrymen gone mad? Who is to blame? And sometimes, walking down a hallway in the college or the newspaper offices, I would ask: How long do you think you can go on like this, Chile? Are you going to change beyond recognition? Become a monster? Then came the elections and Allende won. And I stood before the mirror in my room and tried to formulate the crucial question, which I had saved for just that moment, and the question refused to emerge from my bloodless lips. It was absolutely unbearable. The night of Allende's victory I went out and walked all the way to Farewell's house. He opened the door himself. How old he looked. He must have been about eighty by then, or older, and he had stopped touching my belt or my hips each time we met. Come in, Sebastián, he said. I followed him into the living room. Farewell was making phone calls. The first person he called was Neruda. He couldn't get through. Then he called Nicanor Parra. Engaged too. I collapsed into a chair and covered my face with my hands. I could hear Farewell ringing the numbers of four or five other poets, without any luck. We started drinking. I suggested he ring up some Catholic poets we both knew, if that was going to make him feel better. They're the worst, said Farewell, they're probably all out in the street, celebrating Allende's victory. After a few hours Farewell fell asleep in his chair. I tried to put him to bed, but he was too heavy, so I left him there. When I got back to my house, I went straight to my Greek classics. Let God's will be done, I said. I'm going to reread the Greeks. Respecting the tradition, I started with Homer, then moved on to Thales of Miletus, Xenophanes of Colophon, Alcmaeon of Croton, Zeno of Elea (wonderful), and then a pro-Allende general was killed, and Chile restored diplomatic relations with Cuba and the national census recorded a total of 8,884,746 Chileans and the first episodes of the soap opera *The Right to be Born* were broadcast on television, and I read Tyrtaios of Sparta and Archilochos of Paros and Solon of Athens and Hipponax of Ephesos and Stesichoros of Himnera and Sappho of Mytilene and Ana-kreon of Teos and Pindar of Thebes (one of my favorites), and the government nationalized the copper mines and then the nitrate and steel industries and Pablo Neruda won the Nobel Prize and Díaz Casanueva won the National Literature Prize and Fidel Castro came on a visit and many people thought he would stay and live in Chile for ever and Pérez Zujovic the Christian Democrat ex-minister was killed and Lafourcade published *White Dove* and I gave it a good review, you might say I hailed it in glowing terms, although deep down I knew it wasn't much of a book, and the first anti-Allende march was organized, with people banging pots and pans, and I read Aes-chylus and Sophocles and Euripides, all the tragedies, and Al-kaios of Mytilene and Aesop and Hesiod and Herodotus (a titan among authors), and in Chile there were shortages and inflation and black marketeering and long lines for food and Farewell's estate was expropriated in the Land Reform along with many others and the Bureau of Women's Affairs was set up and Allende went to Mexico and visited the seat of the United Nations in New York and there were terrorist attacks and I read Thucydides, the long wars of Thucydides, the rivers and plains, the winds and the plateaus that traverse the time-darkened pages of Thucydides, and the men he describes, the warriors with their arms, and the civilians, harvesting grapes, or looking from a mountainside at the distant horizon, the horizon where I was just one among millions of beings still to be born, the far-off horizon Thucydides glimpsed and me there trembling indistinguishably, and I also reread Demos-thenes and Menander and Aristotle and Plato (whom one can-not read too often), and there were strikes and the colonel of a tank regiment tried to mount a coup, and a cameraman recorded his own death on film, and then Allende's naval aide-de-camp was assassinated and there were riots, swearing, Chileans blaspheming, painting on walls, and then nearly half a million people marched in support of Allende, and then came the coup d'état, the putsch, the military uprising, the bombing of La Moneda and when the bombing was finished, the president committed suicide and that put an end to it all. I sat there in silence, a finger between the pages to mark my place, and I thought: Peace at last. I got up and looked out the window: Peace and quiet. The sky was blue, a deep, clean blue, with a few scattered clouds. I saw a helicopter in the distance. Leaving the window open, I knelt and prayed, for Chile, for all Chileans, the living and the dead. Then I rang Farewell. How are you feeling? I asked him. I'm dancing a jig, he said. The following days were strange. It was as if until then we had all been dreaming and had suddenly woken to real life, although occasionally it seemed to be the other way round, as if we had all been plunged into a dream. And we went on living day by day in accordance with the abnormal conventions of the dream world: anything can happen and whatever happens the dreamer *accepts* it. Movement works differently. We move like gazelles or the way gazelles move in a tiger's dream. We move like a painting by Vasarely. We move as if we had no shadows and were unperturbed by that appalling fact. We speak. We eat. But underneath we are trying not to realize that we are speaking and eating. One night I found out that Neruda had died. I rang Farewell. Pablo's dead, I said. He died of cancer, said Farewell, cancer. Yes, cancer, I said. Should we go to the funeral? I'm going, said Farewell. I'll go with you, I said. After I hung up, I felt as if I had dreamed the whole conversation. The next day we went to the cemetery. Farewell was very elegantly dressed. He looked like a phantom ship, but very elegant. They're going to give me back my estate, he whispered into my ear. It was a large funeral cortege and people kept joining it as we proceeded. Look at those gorgeous boys! said Farewell. Control yourself, I said. I looked him in the face: Farewell was winking at some strangers. They were young and seemed to be in a bad mood, but at the time I felt they had sprung from a dream in which good and bad moods were no more than metaphysical accidents. I could hear someone behind us who had recognized Farewell saying, That's Farewell, the critic. Words emerging from one dream and entering another. Then someone started shouting. Hysterically. Other hysterics joined in the chant. What's this vulgar carrying-on? asked Farewell. Just some riffraff, I replied, don't worry, it's not far to the cemetery now. And what has become of Pablo? asked Farewell. He's up front, in the coffin, I said. Don't be an idiot, said Farewell, I haven't gone completely gaga yet. I'm sorry, I said. It's all right, he replied. What a pity they don't do funerals like they used to, said Farewell. Indeed, I said. A proper send-off, with eulogies and so forth, said Farewell. In the French manner, I said. I would have written a lovely speech for Pablo, said Farewell, and he started to cry. We must be dreaming, I thought. As we were leaving the cemetery, arm in arm, I saw a man propped against a tomb, asleep. A shiver ran down my spine. The following days were fairly calm, and I was tired from reading all those Greeks. So I returned to the literature of Chile. I tried to write a few poems. For a start everything came out in iambic meter. Then I don't know what came over me. My poetry veered from the angelic to the demonic. Often in the evening I was tempted to show my confessor the verses I had written, but I never did. I wrote about women, hatefully, cruelly, I wrote about homosexuals and children lost in derelict railway stations. If I had to describe my poetry, I would say that, until then, it had always been Apollonian, yet I had begun to write in what might tentatively be described as a Dionysiac mode. But in fact it wasn't Dionysiac poetry. Or demonic poetry. It was just raving mad. Those poor women who appeared in my poems, what had they ever done to me? Deceived me perhaps? What had those poor homosexuals done to me? Nothing. Nothing. Not the women, not the queers. And the children, for God's sake, what could they possibly have done? So what were those hapless creatures doing there, stranded in those landscapes of decay? Maybe I was one of those children? Maybe they were the children I would never have? Maybe they were the lost children of lost parents I would never know? So why was I raving on and on? My daily life, by contrast, was perfectly calm. I spoke in measured tones, never got angry, was organized and punctual. I prayed each night and fell asleep without difficulty. Occasionally I had nightmares, but in those days just about everybody had nightmares from time to time, though some more often than others. In the mornings, nevertheless, I woke up refreshed, ready to face the day's tasks. One particular morning, I was informed that some visitors were waiting for me in the living room. I finished washing and went down. I saw Mr. Raef sitting on a wooden bench against the wall. Mr. Etah was standing with his hands clasped behind his back examining a picture by a painter who claimed to be an expressionist (although he was in fact an impressionist). When they saw me, both of them smiled as one might smile at an old friend. I invited them to join me for breakfast. To my surprise, they said they had broken their fast some time before, although according to the clock on the wall it was just a few minutes past eight. They agreed to have a cup of tea, just to keep me company. There's not much more to my breakfast, I said. Black tea, toast with butter and marmalade, orange juice. A balanced breakfast, said Mr. Raef. Mr. Etah didn't say anything. I instructed the maid to serve breakfast on the verandah, which looks out over the garden to the walls of the adjoining college, partly hidden by greenery. We've been sent to make a proposal relating to a very delicate matter, said Mr. Raef. I nodded and remained silent. Mr. Etah had taken one of my slices of toast and was spreading butter on it. It's something that needs to be treated in the strictest confidence, said Mr. Raef, especially now, with the current situation. I said yes, of course, I understood. Mr. Etah took a bite from the slice of toast and looked out at a group of three araucaria trees, the pride of the college, soaring cathedral-like over the gardens. You know what Chileans are like, Fr. Urrutia, always gossiping, not in a nasty way, I don't mean that, but great ones for gossip all the same. I didn't say anything. Mr. Etah finished off the slice of toast in three mouthfuls and started buttering another. Why am I telling you this? Mr. Raef asked himself rhetorically. Well, the matter we've come to see you about requires absolute discretion. I said yes, I understood. Mr. Etah poured himself another cup of tea and clicked his thumb and middle finger to get the maid to bring him some milk. What do you understand? asked Mr. Raef, with a frank and friendly smile. That you require me to be absolutely discreet, I said. More than that, said Mr. Raef, much more, we require ultra-absolute discretion, extraordinarily absolute discretion and secrecy. I was itching to correct him but restrained myself, because I wanted to know what they were proposing. Do you know anything about Marxism? asked Mr. Etah, after wiping his lips with a napkin. A bit, yes, but only out of intellectual curiosity, I said. I mean, I'm not in the least sympathetic to the doctrine, ask anyone. But do you know about it or not? A little bit, I said, feeling increasingly nervous. Do you have any books about Marxism in your library? asked Mr. Etah. Heavens, it's not my library, it belongs to the community, there might be something, but only for reference, to be used as a source for philosophical essays aiming precisely to refute Marxism. But you've got your own library, haven't you, Fr. Urrutia, your own personal, private library so to speak, some books are kept here in the college and others in your house, or your mother's house, isn't that right? Yes, that's right, I murmured. And in your private library are there or are there not books about Marxism? asked Mr. Etah. Please answer yes or no, Mr. Raef implored me. Yes, I said. So could we say that you know something or perhaps more than something about Marxism? asked Mr. Etah fixing me with his penetrating gaze. I looked to Mr. Raef for help. He made a face I couldn't interpret: it might have been expressing solidarity with his colleague or complicity with me. I don't know what to say, I said. Say something, said Mr. Raef. You know me, I'm not a Marxist, I said. But are you familiar or not with, shall we say, the fundamentals of Marxism? asked Mr. Etah. Well, who isn't? I said. So what you're saying is that it's not very hard to learn, said Mr. Etah. No, it's not very hard, I said, trembling from head to toe and feeling more than ever as if it were all a dream. Mr. Raef slapped me on the leg. It was meant to be friendly but I almost jumped out of my skin. If it's not hard to learn, it wouldn't be hard to teach either, said Mr. Etah. I remained silent until it was clear they were waiting for me to say something. No, I said, I guess it wouldn't be very hard to teach.

Although I've never taught it, I added. Now's your chance, said Mr. Etah. You'll be serving your country, said Mr. Raef. Serving in silence and obscurity, far from the glitter of medals, he added. To put it bluntly, you're going to have to keep your mouth shut, said Mr. Etah. Hush-hush, said Mr. Raef. Lips sealed, said Mr. Etah. Silent as the grave, said Mr. Raef. No going around shooting your mouth off about it, you understand, absolute discretion, said Mr. Etah. And just what does this delicate task involve? I asked. Giving some classes on Marxism, not many, just the basics really, to some gentlemen we're all deeply indebted to in this country, said Mr. Raef, leaning forward and exhaling a sewerlike stench in my face. I couldn't help frowning. My expression of displeasure made Mr. Raef smile. Don't rack your brains, you'll never guess who they are. And if I accept, when would these classes start, because right now I have quite a bit of work piled up, I said. Don't get coy with us, said Mr. Etah, this is an offer no one can refuse. An offer no one would want to refuse, said Mr. Raef in a conciliatory tone. I felt the danger was past and the time had come to be firm. Who are my pupils? I asked. General Pinochet, said Mr. Etah. My breath caught in my throat. And the others? General Leigh, Admiral Merino and General Mendoza, of course, who else? said Mr. Raef, lowering his voice. I'll have to prepare myself, I said, this is not something to be taken lightly. The classes have to start within a week, is that enough time for you? I said yes, two weeks would have been better, but I could manage with one. Then Mr. Raef talked about the fee. You'll only be doing your patriotic duty, he said, but everyone's got to eat. I probably agreed with him. I can't remember what else we said. The week went by with the same calm, dreamy feeling as the weeks before. One afternoon, when I was leaving the newspaper office, there was a car waiting for me. I was taken to the college to pick up my notes and then the car plunged into the Santiago night. In the back seat, sitting next to me, was a colonel, Colonel Pérez Latouche, who handed me an envelope which I decided not to open, and stressed once again what Mr. Raef and Mr. Etah had been at such pains to make clear: the importance of absolute discretion with regard to every aspect of my new assignment. I assured him he could count on me. Let's say no more about it then and just enjoy the drive, said Colonel Pérez Latouche, offering me a glass of whiskey, which I declined. Is it because of the cassock? he asked. And only then did I realize that when we had gone to the college I had changed out of the suit I was wearing at the office and put on a cassock. I shook my head. Pérez Latouche said he knew a few priests who were pretty good drinkers. I said I doubted there were any good drinkers in Chile, priests or lay folk. We tend to be bad drinkers in this country. As I expected, Pérez Latouche disagreed. I let him go on and stopped listening, wondering what had prompted me to change my clothes. Was it that I wanted to be in uniform too, so to speak, when facing my illustrious pupils for the first time? Was I afraid of something? Did I feel the cassock would ward off some indefinable, undeniable danger? I tried to open the curtains covering the windows of the car, but could not. There was a metal bar holding them in place. It's a security measure, said Pérez Latouche, who was still listing Chilean wines and incorrigible Chilean drunks, as if he were unwittingly, and ironically, reciting one of Pablo de Rokha's crazy poems. Then the car drove into a garden and stopped in front of a house with only one light on, above the main door. I followed Pérez Latouche. He realized I was looking for the soldiers on guard duty and explained that the best guards were the ones you couldn't see. So there are guards? I asked. Oh yes, and each one has his finger on the trigger. That's good to know, I said. We entered a room where the furniture and the walls were blindingly white. Take a seat, said Pérez Latouche, What would you like to drink? A cup of tea? I suggested. Tea, excellent, said Pérez Latouche, and left the room. I was left standing there on my own. I was sure they were filming me. There were two mirrors with gilded wooden frames that they could easily have been using. I could hear distant voices, people discussing something or sharing a joke. Then silence again. I heard footsteps and a door opening: a waiter dressed in white brought me a cup of tea on a silver tray. I thanked him. He murmured something I didn't catch and vanished. When I was putting sugar in my tea I saw my face reflected in the surface of the liquid. Who would have thought you'd come to this, Sebastián? I said to myself. I felt like flinging the cup at one of those immaculate walls, I felt like sitting down with the cup between my knees and crying, I felt like shrinking until I could dive into the warm infusion and swim to the bottom, where the sugar crystals lay like big chunks of diamond. But I remained hieratic and expressionless. I put on a bored look. I stirred my tea and tasted it. It was good. Good tea. Good for the nerves. Then I heard steps in the corridor, not the corridor by which I had arrived, but another one, leading to a door right in front of me. The door opened and in came the aides-de-camp or adjutants, all of them in uniform, then a group of batmen or young officers, and then the Junta in full made its entrance. I got to my feet. From the corner of my eye I could see myself reflected in a mirror. The uniforms shimmered a moment like shiny cardboard cutouts, then like a restless forest. My black, loose-fitting cassock seemed to absorb the whole spectrum of colors in an instant. That first night we talked about Marx and Engels. How they came to work together. Then we looked at the *Manifesto of the Communist Party* and the *Address of the Central Committee to the Communist League*. For background reading I gave them the *Manifesto* and *Basic Elements of Historical Materialism*, by our compatriot Marta Harnecker. In the second class, a week later, we discussed *The Class Struggles in France: 1848–1850* and *The Eighteenth Brumaire of Louis Bonaparte*, and Admiral Merino asked if I was personally acquainted with Marta Harnecker, and if so, what I thought of her. I said I didn't know her personally, I explained that she was a disciple of Althusser (he didn't know who Althusser was, so I told him), and had studied in France, like many Chileans. Is she good-looking? I believe she is, I said. In the third class we returned to the *Manifesto*. According to General Leigh it was an unadulterated urtext. He didn't elaborate. At first I thought he was making fun of me, but it soon became clear that he was serious. I'll have to think about that later, I said to myself. General Pinochet seemed to be very tired. This was the first class to which he had come in uniform. He spent it slumped in an armchair, jotting down the odd note, not once removing his dark glasses. I think he fell asleep for a few minutes, still firmly gripping his propelling pencil. Of the Junta, only General Pinochet and General Mendoza were present at the fourth class. Seeing me hesitate, General Pinochet gave the order to proceed as if the others were there as well, and, in a symbolic way, they were, since among those present I recognized a Navy captain and an Air Force general. I talked about *Capital* (I had prepared a three-page summary) and *The Civil War in France*. General Mendoza didn't ask a single question in the whole class, he just took notes. There were several copies of *Basic Elements of Historical Materialism* on the desk, and when the class was over General Pinochet told the others to take a copy away with them. He winked at me and shook my hand warmly before leaving. I never saw him in such a genial mood. In the fifth class I talked about *Wages, Price and Profit* and discussed the *Manifesto* again. After an hour General Mendoza was sleeping soundly. Don't worry, said General Pinochet, come with me. I followed him to a large window, which looked out over the gardens behind the house. A full moon illuminated the smooth surface of a swimming pool. He opened the window. Behind us I could hear the muffled voices of the generals talking about Marta Harnecker. A delicious perfume given off by clumps of flowers was wafting all through the gardens. A bird called out and straightaway, from somewhere within the walls or from an adjoining property, a bird of the same species replied, then I heard a flapping of wings that seemed to rip through the night and then the deep silence returned, unscathed. Let's take a walk, said the general. As if he were a magician, as soon as we stepped through the window frame and entered the enchanted gardens, lights came on, exquisitely scattered here and there among the plants. Then I talked about *The Origin of the Family, Private Property and the State*, which Engels wrote on his own, and the General nodded at each stage of my explanation, now and then asking a pertinent question, and from time to time both of us fell silent and looked at the moon sailing on alone through infinite space. Perhaps it was that vision that gave me the nerve to ask him if he knew Leopardi. He said he didn't. He asked who Leopardi was. We stopped for a moment. Standing at the window, the other generals were looking out into the night. A nineteenth-century Italian poet, I said. If I may be so bold, sir, I said, this moon reminds me of two of his poems: "The Infinite" and "Night Song of a Wandering Shepherd of Asia." General Pinochet did not express the slightest interest. Walking beside him I recited what I knew by heart of "The Infinite." Nice poetry, he said. In the sixth class everyone was present again: General Leigh struck me as something of a star pupil, Admiral Merino was a fine and, above all, a friendly conversationalist, while General Mendoza, true to form, remained silent and took notes. We talked about Marta Harnecker. General Leigh said that the young woman in question was intimately acquainted with a pair of Cubans. The admiral confirmed this report. Is that possible? said General Pinochet. Can that be possible? Are we talking about a woman or a bitch? Is this information correct? It is, said Leigh. Suddenly I had an idea for a poem about a degenerate woman, and I made a mental note of the first lines and the general drift that night while talking about *Basic Elements of Historical Materialism* and going back over some points from the *Manifesto* that they still hadn't properly grasped. In the seventh class I talked about Lenin and Stalin and Trotsky and the various rival schools of Marxism around the world. I talked about Mao and Tito and Fidel Castro. All of them (except General Mendoza who wasn't there for the seventh class) had read *Basic Elements of Historical Materialism*, and when the discussion started to flag we went back to talking about Marta Harnecker. I remember we also discussed Chairman Mao's military accomplishments. General Pinochet said that the really gifted strategist in that part of the world was not Mao but another Chinaman, whose unpronounceable names he mentioned, but of course I forgot them straightaway. General Leigh said that Marta Harnecker was probably working for the Cuban secret service. Is this information correct? It is. In the eighth class I talked about Lenin again and we examined *What Is to Be Done?* and then we went over Mao's *Little Red Book* (which General Pinochet found very simple and straightforward), and then we came back to *Basic Elements of Historical Materialism*, by Marta Harnecker. In the ninth class I asked them questions about Harnecker's *Basic Elements*. Overall, the answers were satisfactory. The tenth class was the last. Only General Pinochet came. We talked about religion rather than politics. When it was over, he gave me a gift on behalf of himself and the other members of the Junta. I don't know why, but I had expected the goodbye to be more personal. It was rather cold, though perfectly polite of course, in strict accordance with state protocol. I asked him if the classes had been useful. Of course, said the general. I asked if I had lived up to their expectations. You may go with a clear conscience, he assured me, you've done a splendid job. Colonel Pérez Latouche accompanied me home. When I got there, at two in the morning, after driving through the empty streets of Santiago, reduced to geometry by the curfew, I couldn't get to sleep and didn't know what to do. I started walking up and down in my room while a rising tide of images and voices crowded into my brain. Ten classes, I said to myself. Only nine, really. Nine classes. Nine lessons. Not much of a bibliography. Was it all right? Did they learn anything? Did I teach them anything? Did I do what I had to do? Did I do what I ought to have done? Is Marxism a kind of humanism? Or a diabolical theory? If I told my literary friends what I had done, would they approve? Would some condemn my actions out of hand? Would some understand and forgive me? Is it *always* possible for a man to know what is good and what is bad? In the midst of these deliberations, I broke down and began to cry helplessly, stretched out on the bed, blaming Mr. Raef and Mr. Etah for my misfortunes (in an intellectual sense) since they were the ones who got me into that business in the first place. Then, before I knew it, I was asleep. That week I dined with Farewell. I could no longer bear the weight, or to be perhaps more precise, the alternatively pendular and circular oscillations of my conscience, and the phosphorescent mist, glowing dimly like a marsh at the vesperal hour, through which my lucidity had to make its way, dragging the rest of me along. So when Farewell and I were having pre-dinner drinks, I told him. In spite of Colonel Pérez Latouche's stern warnings about absolute discretion, I told him about my strange adventure, teaching that secret group of illustrious pupils. And Farewell, who until then had seemed to be floating in the monosyllabic apathy to which he was increasingly prone with age, pricked up his ears and begged me to tell the whole story, leaving nothing out. And that is what I did, I told him about how I had been contacted, about the house in Las Condes where the classes took place, the positive reactions of my students, who were most attentive, and unfailingly curious, in spite of the fact that some of the lessons took place late at night, the stipend I received for my labors, and other minor details it is hardly worth even trying to remember now. And then Farewell looked at me, narrowing his eyes, as if I had suddenly become a stranger to him or he had discovered another face behind my face or was suffering an attack of bitter envy, provoked by my unexpected visit to the corridors of power, and, in a voice that seemed oddly clipped, as if in that state he could only manage to get half the question out, he asked me what General Pinochet was like. And I shrugged my shoulders, as people do in novels, but never in real life. And Farewell said: A man like that, he must have something that makes him stand out. And I shrugged my shoulders again. And Farewell said: Think, Sebastián, in a tone of voice that might just as well have accompanied other words, such as Think, you little shit of a priest. And I shrugged my shoulders and pretended to be thinking. And with a sort of senile ferocity Farewell's narrowed eyes kept trying to bore into mine. And then I remembered the first time I had a more or less one-to-one conversation with the general, before the third or fourth class, a few minutes before the start, I was sitting there balancing a cup of tea on my knees and the general, stately and imposing in uniform, came up to me and asked if I knew what Allende used to read. And I put the teacup on the tray and stood up. And the general said, Sit down, Father. Or perhaps he didn't actually say anything but indicated that I should sit with a gesture. Then he made a remark about the class that was about to begin, something about a corridor with high walls, something about a throng of pupils. And I smiled beatifically and sat down. And then the general asked me the question, if I knew what Allende read, if I thought Allende was an intellectual. And, caught by surprise, I didn't know how to answer, as I confessed to Farewell. And the general said to me: Everyone's presenting him as a martyr and an intellectual now, because plain martyrs are not so interesting any more, are they? And I tilted my head and smiled beatifically. But he wasn't an intellectual, unless you can call someone who doesn't read or study an intellectual, said the general, What do you think? I shrugged my shoulders like a wounded bird. But you can't, can you? said the general. If someone doesn't read or study, he's not an intellectual, any fool can see that. And what do you think Allende used to read? I moved my head slightly and smiled. Magazines. All he read was magazines. Summaries of books. Articles his followers used to cut out for him. I have it from a reliable source, believe me. I always suspected as much, I whispered. Well, your suspicions were well founded. And what do you think Frei read? I don't know, sir, I murmured, with a little more assurance. Nothing. He didn't read at all. Not a word, not even the Bible. How does that strike you, as a priest? I'm not sure I have a firm opinion on the matter, sir, I mumbled. I would have thought one of the founders of the Christian Democrats could at least read the Bible, wouldn't you? said the general. Perhaps, I stammered. I'm just pointing it out, I don't mean to be hostile, it's just an observation, it's a fact and I'm pointing it out, I'm not drawing any conclusions, not yet anyway, am I? No, I said. And Alessandri? Have you ever wondered what books Alessandri read? No sir, I whispered, smiling. Well, he read romances. President Alessandri read romances, I ask you, romances, what do you think of that? It's amazing, sir. Although of course, it's what one would have expected from Alessandri, or at least it makes sense that he should have been drawn to that sort of reading matter. Do you see what I'm getting at? I'm afraid I don't, sir, I said, looking pained. Well, poor old Alessandri, said General Pinochet, fixing me with his gaze. Oh, of course, I said. Do you see now? Yes I do, sir, I said. Can you remember a single article he wrote, something he actually wrote himself, as opposed to what his hacks used to turn out? I don't think I can, sir, I murmured. Of course you can't, because he never wrote anything. And the same goes for Frei and Allende. They didn't read, they didn't write. They pretended to be cultured, but not one of them was a reader or a writer. Maybe they knew something about the press, but they knew nothing about books.

Indeed, sir, quite, I said, smiling beatifically. And then the general said: How many books do you think I've written? My blood ran cold, as I said to Farewell. I had no idea. Three or four, said Farewell confidently. In any case I just didn't know. And I had to admit it. Three, said the general. But the thing is they have all been with little-known or specialist publishers. But drink your tea, Father, or it'll get cold. What a wonderful surprise, I said, I didn't know. Well, they're military books, military history, geopolitics, aimed at a specialist readership. That's marvellous, three books, I said, my voice faltering. And I've published countless articles in journals, even in North America, translated into English, of course. I would love to read one of your books, sir, I whispered. Go to the National Library, they're all there. I'll be there tomorrow, without fail, I said. The general didn't seem to have heard. Nobody helped me, I wrote them all on my own, three books, one of them quite a thick book, with no help, burning the midnight oil. And then he said: Countless articles, on all sorts of topics, but always of course related to military matters. For a while we sat there in silence, although I kept nodding the whole time, as if inviting him to go on talking. Why do you think I'm telling you all this? he said, out of the blue. I shrugged my shoulders and smiled beatifically. To avoid any misunderstanding, he declared. So you know I'm an avid reader, I read books about history and political theory, I even read novels. The last one I read was *White Dove* by Lafourcade, very much a book for the younger generation, but I'm not one of those snobs who never looks at anything new, so I read it, and I enjoyed it. Have you read it? Yes sir, I said. And what did you think? It's excellent, sir, in fact I reviewed it in quite glowing terms. Well it's nothing to get carried away about either, said Pinochet. No, not carried away, I said. And there we sat in silence again. Suddenly the General put his hand on my knee, I said to Farewell. A shiver ran down my spine. For a moment my mind was prey to a surging multitude of hands. Why do you think I want to learn about the fundamentals of Marxism? he asked. The better to serve our country, sir. Exactly, in order to understand Chile's enemies, to find out how they think, to get an idea of how far they are prepared to go. I know how far I am prepared to go myself, I assure you. But I also want to know how far they are prepared to go. And I'm not afraid of studying. One should aim to learn something new every day. I'm always reading and writing. All the time. Which is more than you could say for Allende or Frei or Alessandri, isn't it? I nodded three times. So what I'm saying, Father, is that you won't be wasting your time with me, and I won't be wasting my time with you, will I? Absolutely not, sir, I said. And when I finished telling this story, Farewell was still staring at me, his half closed eyes like empty bear traps ruined by time and rain and freezing cold. It was as if Chile's great twentieth-century literary critic were dead. Farewell, I whispered, Did I do the right thing or not? And since there was no reply, I repeated the question: Did I do my duty, or did I go beyond it? And Farewell replied with another question: Was it a necessary or an unnecessary course of action? Necessary, necessary, necessary, I said. That seemed to satisfy him, and me too, at the time. And then we went on eating and talking. And at some point in our conversation, I said to him: Not a word to anyone about what I told you. It goes without saying, said Farewell, in a tone of voice that reminded me of Colonel Pérez Latouche. Quite different from the rather ungentlemanly tone Mr. Raef and Mr. Etah had used a few days before. In any case, the following week, a ru-

mor began to spread like wildfire around Santiago. Father Ibacache had given the Junta lessons in Marxism. When I found
out, my blood ran cold. I saw Farewell, I mean I imagined the
scene so clearly I could have been spying on him, sitting in his
favorite easy chair or armchair at the club or in the salon of
some old crone whose friendship he had been cultivating for
decades, holding court, half gaga, surrounded by retired generals who had gone into business, queers in English suits, ladies
with illustrious names and one foot in the grave, sitting there
blabbing out the story of how I was engaged as the Junta's
private tutor. And the queers and moribund crones and even
the retired generals turned business consultants wasted no
time in telling the story to others, who told it to others, and
so on. Naturally, Farewell claimed he was not the motor or the
fuse or the match that had started the gossiping, and as it was
I had neither the strength nor the desire to blame him. So I
sat down beside the telephone and waited for my friends or
my former friends to call, or Mr. Etah, Mr. Raef and Pérez
Latouche, to reproach me for being indiscreet, or anonymous
callers with axes to grind, or the ecclesiastical authorities ringing to find out just how much truth and how much fabrication
there was in the rumors that had spread through Santiago's
literary and artistic circles, if not beyond, but no one called.
At first I thought this silence was the result of a concerted de-
cision to ostracize me. Then, to my astonishment, I realized
that nobody gave a damn. The country was populated by hieratic figures, heading implacably towards an unfamiliar, gray
horizon, where one could barely glimpse a few rays of light,
flashes of lightning and clouds of smoke. What lay there? We
did not know. No Sordello. That much was clear. No Guido.
No leafy trees. No trotting horses. No discussion or research.

Perhaps we were heading towards our souls, or the tormented souls of our forefathers, towards the endless plain spread before our sleepy or tearful eyes, our spent or humiliated eyes, by all the good and bad things we and others had done. So it was hardly surprising that nobody cared about my introductory course on Marxism. Sooner or later everyone would get their share of power again. The right, the center and the left, one big happy family. A couple of ethical problems, admittedly. But no aesthetic problems at all. Now we have a socialist president and life is exactly the same. The Communists (who go on as if the Berlin Wall hadn't come down), the Christian Democrats, the Socialists, the right and the military. Or the other way round. I could just as well say it the other way round! The order of the factors doesn't alter the product! No problems! Just a little bout of fever! Just three acts of madness! Just an unusually prolonged psychotic episode! Once again I could go out, I could ring people up and no one made any remarks. Throughout those years of steel and silence, many people actually praised me for resolutely continuing to publish my reviews and articles. Many praised my poetry! Several came to ask me for favors! I was generous with letters of recommendation and references, performing various Chilean leg ups of little consequence, which earned me the undying gratitude of my beneficiaries. At the end of the day, we were all reasonable (except for the wizened youth, who at that stage was wandering around God knows where, lost in some black hole or other), we were all Chileans, we were all normal, discreet, logical, balanced, careful, sensible people, we all knew that something had to be done, that certain things were *necessary*, there's a time for sacrifice and a time for thinking reasonably. Sometimes, at night, I would sit on a chair in the dark and ask myself what difference there was between fascist and rebel. Just a pair of words. Two words, that's all. And sometimes either one will do! So I went out into the street and breathed the air of Santiago with the vague conviction that I was living, if not in the best of worlds, at least in a *possible* world, a *real* world, and I published a book of poems that struck even me as odd, I mean it was odd that I should have written them, they were odd coming from me, but I published them in the name of freedom, my own and that of my readers, and then I went back to giving classes and lectures, and I published another book in Spain, in Pamplona, and then it was my turn to frequent the airports of the world, mingling with elegant Europeans and serious (and weary-looking) North Americans, mingling with the best-dressed men of Italy, Germany, France and England, gentlemen whom it was a pleasure simply to behold, and there I was, with my cassock fluttering in the air-conditioned breeze or the gusts that issue from automatic doors when they open suddenly, for no logical reason, as if they had a presentiment of God's presence, and, seeing my humble cassock flapping, people would say, There goes Fr. Sebastián, there goes Fr. Urrutia, that splendid Chilean, and then I returned to Chile, for I always return, how else would I merit the appellation *splendid Chilean*, and I went on writing reviews for the newspaper, and critical articles crying out for a different approach to culture, as even the most inattentive reader could hardly fail to notice if he scratched the surface a little, critical articles crying out, indeed begging, for a return to the Greek and Latin greats, to the Troubadours, to the *dolce stil nuovo* and the classics of Spain, France and England, more culture! more culture! read Whitman and Pound and Eliot, read Neruda and Borges and Vallejo, read Victor Hugo, for

God's sake, and Tolstoy, and proudly I cried myself hoarse in the desert, but my vociferations and on occasions my howling could only be heard by those who were able to scratch the surface of my writings with the nails of their index fingers, and they were not many, but enough for me, and life went on and on and on, like a necklace of rice grains, on each grain of which a landscape had been painted, tiny grains and microscopic landscapes, and I knew that everyone was putting that necklace on and wearing it, but no one had the patience or the strength or the courage to take it off and look at it closely and decipher each landscape grain by grain, partly because to do so required the vision of a lynx or an eagle, and partly because the landscapes usually turned out to contain unpleasant surprises like coffins, makeshift cemeteries, ghost towns, the void and the horror, the smallness of being and its ridiculous will, people watching television, people going to football matches, boredom circumnavigating the Chilean imagination like an enormous aircraft carrier. And that's the truth. We were bored. We read and we got bored. We intellectuals. Because you can't read all day and all night. You can't write all day and all night. Splendid isolation has never been our style, and back then, as now, Chilean artists and writers needed to gather and talk, ideally in a pleasant setting where they could find intelligent company. Apart from the inescapable fact that many of the old crowd had left the country for reasons that were often more personal than political, the main difficulty was the curfew. Where could the artists and intellectuals meet if everywhere was shut after ten at night, for, as everyone knows, night is the most propitious time for getting together and enjoying a little unbuttoned conversation with one's peers. Artists and writers. Strange times. I can picture the wizened youth's face. I cannot actually see him, but he is there in my mind's eye. He is wrinkling his nose, scanning the horizon, shaking from head to foot. I cannot actually see him, but there he is in my mind's eye, crouching or down on all fours, on a hillock, black clouds racing past over his head, and the hillock becomes a hill and the next minute it is the atrium of a church, an atrium as black as the clouds, charged with electricity like the clouds, and glistening with moisture or blood, and the wizened youth trembles more and more violently, wrinkles his nose and then pounces on the story. But only I know the story, the real story. And it is simple and cruel and true and it should make us laugh, it should make us die laughing. But we only know how to cry, the only thing we do wholeheartedly is cry. The curfew was in force. Restaurants and bars shut early. People went home at a prudent hour. There were not many places where writers and artists could gather to drink and talk as long as they liked. That's the truth. So this is how it happened. There was a woman. Her name was María Canales. She was a writer, she was pretty, she was young. In my opinion she was not without talent. I thought so then, and still do. Her talent was, how can I put it? inward, sheathed, withdrawn. Others have recanted, they have put it all behind them and forgotten. Naked, the wizened youth lunges at his prey. But I know the story of María Canales, the whole story, everything that happened. She was a writer. Maybe she still is. Writers (and critics) didn't have many places to go. María Canales had a house on the outskirts of the city. A big house, surrounded by a garden full of trees, a house with a comfortable sitting room, with a fireplace and good whiskey, good cognac, a house that was open to friends once or twice a week, even occasionally three times a week. I don't know how we got to know her. I suppose one day she showed up at the editorial office of a newspaper or a literary magazine or at the Chilean Society of Authors. She probably attended a writing workshop. In any case before long we all knew her and she knew all of us. She was pleasant company. As I said before, she was pretty. She had brown hair and large eyes and she read everything she was told to read or so she led us to believe. She went to exhibitions. Maybe we met her at an exhibition. Maybe at the end of a vernissage she invited people to continue the party at her house. She was pretty, as I said. She was interested in art, she liked to talk with painters and performance artists and video artists, maybe because they were not as well educated as the writers. Or so she thought. Then she began to mix with writers and realized that they were not particularly well educated either. What a relief that must have been. A very Chilean sort of relief. So few of us are truly cultured in this godforsaken country. The rest are completely ignorant. Pleasant, likeable people all the same. María Canales was pleasant and likeable: she was a generous host, nothing was too much trouble when it came to making her guests feel at home, for that, it seemed, was what mattered most to her. And people really did feel comfortable at the select gatherings or receptions or soirées or parties hosted by the novice writer. She had two sons. I haven't mentioned them yet. If I remember rightly, she had two young sons, the elder was two or three years old and the younger about eight months, and she was married to a North American called James Thompson, whom she referred to as Jimmy, who worked as a salesman or an executive for a firm that had recently set up a branch in Chile and another in Argentina. Naturally, everyone got to meet Jimmy. I met him too. He was a typical North American, tall, with brown hair slightly lighter in color than his wife's, not very talkative but polite. Sometimes he was present at María's get-togethers and on those occasions he was generally to be seen listening to one of the duller guests with infinite patience. By the time the visitors arrived, and emerged from the cheerful caravan of miscellaneous automobiles, the boys would be asleep in their room on the second floor, it was a three-story house, and sometimes the maid or the nanny would carry them downstairs in their pajamas, to say hello to the newly arrived guests and be subjected to their baby talk and remarks about how cute or well behaved they were, or how much they looked like their mother or their father, although to tell the truth, the elder boy, who was called Sebastián, like me, didn't look like either of his parents, as opposed to the younger boy, named Jimmy, who was the spitting image of Jimmy senior, with a few South American features inherited from María Canales. Then the children would disappear along with the maid, who shut herself away in the room next to theirs, while downstairs, in María Canales's spacious sitting room, the party would begin in earnest, with the hostess serving whiskies all round, Debussy on the record player, or Webern performed by the Berlin Philharmonic, and after a while someone would be moved to recite a poem, and someone else would weigh up the virtues of this or that novel, the conversation would turn to painting or contemporary dance, little groups would form, the latest work by so-and-so would take a hiding, but wasn't what's-his-name's recent performance a delight, the yawning would begin, sometimes a young poet opposed to the regime would come up to me and start talking about Pound and end up talking about his own work (I was always interested in the work of the younger generation, whatever their political affiliations), the hostess would suddenly appear carrying a tray piled high with empanadas, someone would start crying, others would burst into song, at six in the morning, or seven, when the curfew was over, we would make our unsteady way back to the cars in Indian file, some in pairs, others half asleep, most of us happy, and then the motors of six or seven cars would startle the quiet morning, and for a few seconds drown out the sound of birdsong in the garden, and the hostess would wave goodbye from the porch, as the cars began to drive away, one of us having opened the iron gate, and María Canales would stand there on the porch until the last car had left her property, her hospitable domain, and the cars went off down the empty avenues of outer Santiago, those endless avenues, lined with solitary houses, abandoned or neglected villas and vacant lots, their profiles repeated over and over on either side, while the sun came up over the Cordillera and we heard the dissonant rumor of a new day coming from the hub of the city. And a week later we would be back there again. By we I mean the group. I didn't go every week. I put in an appearance chez María Canales once a month. Or even less often. But there were writers who went every week. Or more! They all deny it now. They even claim I was the true habitué, present every week without fail. Or twice, three times a week! But even the wizened youth knows that is patently false. So we can rule that out straightaway. My visits were rare. Infrequent, at worst. But when I did go, I kept my wits about me, and the whiskey didn't cloud my judgement. For example I noticed that young Sebastián, my little namesake, looked rather drawn. One day the maid brought him downstairs, and I took him from her arms and asked what was wrong with him. The maid, who was a full-blood Mapuche, stared at me and tried to take the child back. I ducked away. What's wrong, Sebastián? I said, with a tenderness I had never felt before. The child looked at me with his big blue eyes. I touched his face. What a cold little face it was. Suddenly I felt my eyes brimming with tears. Then the maid snatched him away from me in a most ungracious manner. I wanted to tell her that I was a priest. But something stopped me, perhaps that sense we Chileans possess to an uncommon degree, the sharpest of all our senses, the sense of the ridiculous. When the maid carried the little boy upstairs again, he looked at me over her shoulder and it seemed to me that those wide eyes were seeing something they did not want to see. María Canales was very proud of him: she told me how intelligent he was. The younger son, she said, was wonderfully inquisitive and bold. I didn't pay much attention: all mothers prattle on like that. Mainly I talked with the up-and-coming artists, who, armed with nothing but what they had gleaned from a few books read in secret, were preparing to create the New Chilean Scene, a rather awkward anglicism invented to name the gap left by the emigrants, which my fellow guests were planning to occupy and populate with their as yet embryonic works. I talked with them and with old friends from years back who turned up from time to time (like me) in the house on the outskirts of Santiago to discuss English metaphysical poetry or the films they had seen recently in New York. I can't have had more than about two conversations with María Canales, just short chats really, and once I read a story she had written, a story that went on to win first prize in a competition organized by a left-leaning literary magazine. I remember that competition. I wasn't on the judging panel. They didn't even ask me. If they had asked me, I would have done it. Literature is literature. But anyhow I wasn't one of the judges. Perhaps if I had been, María Canales wouldn't have won first prize. Not that it was a positively bad story, but it certainly wasn't good. Like its author, it was laborious and mediocre. When I showed it to Farewell, who was still alive at the time, although he never attended a literary gathering at María Canales's house, mostly because by then he rarely went out or talked with anyone except his faithful crones, when I showed it to him, he read a couple of lines and said it was frightful, unworthy of a prize even in Bolivia, and then he launched into a bitter lament about the state of Chilean literature, was there one contemporary writer you could seriously compare to Rafael Maluenda, Juan de Armaza or Guillermo Labarca Hubertson? Farewell was sitting in his armchair, and I was sitting opposite him, in the armchair reserved for close friends. I remember shutting my eyes and hanging my head. Who remembers Juan de Armaza now? I thought as night fell with a snakelike hissing. Only Farewell and some old crone with an elephantine memory. A professor of literature in some remote southern town. A crazy grandson, living in a perfect, inexistent past. We have nothing, I murmured. What did you say? said Farewell. Nothing, I said. Are you feeling all right? asked Farewell. Fine, I said. And then I said or thought: Two conversations. And I said or thought it at Farewell's house, which was falling apart like its owner, or back in my monkish cell. Because I only had two conversations with María Canales. At her soirées I would usually sit in a corner, near the stairs, beside a large window, next to a table on which there was always an earthenware vase with fresh flowers in it, and I stayed put in that corner, and there I talked with the desperate poet, the feminist novelist and the avant-garde painter, always keeping an eye on the staircase, waiting for the ritual descent of the Mapuche maid and little Sebastián. And sometimes María Canales joined my group. Always so pleasant! Whatever I wanted, nothing was too much trouble. But I suspect she could hardly understand a thing I said. She pretended to understand, but how could she have? And she could hardly understand the poet's ideas either, although she had a slightly better grasp of the novelist's concerns, and was positively enthusiastic about the painter's schemes. For the most part, however, she just listened. That is, at least, when she was in my corner, in my exclusive little clique. In the other groups scattered around that spacious sitting room, she was, as a rule, the one who called the shots. And when she talked politics she was absolutely sure of herself, and her voice rang out clearly, making her opinions known in no uncertain terms. In spite of which she never ceased to be a model hostess: she knew how to ease any tension with a joke or some playful Chilean teasing. On one occasion she came over to me (I was alone, a glass of whiskey in my hand, thinking about little Sebastián and his wan little face) and without any preliminaries began singing the praises of the feminist novelist. The way she writes, it's quite unique, she said. I replied frankly: many passages in her books were poor translations (I preferred not to speak of plagiarism, which is always a harsh if not an unjust term) of certain French women writers of the fifties. I watched her expression. There was, undeniably, a certain native cunning in that face of hers. She looked at me blankly and then, little by little, almost imperceptibly, a smile, or the irrepressible prelude to a smile, slightly rearranged her features. Nobody else would have picked it for a smile, but I'm a Catholic priest and I knew straightaway. It was harder to tell what kind of smile it was. Perhaps it was a smile of satisfaction, but what was she satisfied about? Perhaps it was a smile of recognition, as if those words had revealed my true face and now she *knew* (or oh so cunningly thought she did, at least) who I really was, or perhaps it was just an empty smile, the sort of smile that forms mysteriously out of nothing and dissolves away into nothing again. In other words you don't like her books, she said. The smile disappeared and her face went blank and dull again. Of course I like them, I replied, I'm just critically noting their weaknesses. What an absurd thing to say. That's what I think now, lying here, confined to this bed, my poor old skeleton propped up on one elbow. How trivial, how grammatically awkward, how plain stupid. We all have weaknesses, I said. How dreadful. Only works of genius will prove to be unblemished. How ghastly. My elbow is shaking. My bed is shaking. The sheets and the blankets are shaking. Where is the wizened youth? He's probably finding it all very funny, the story of my bungling. He's probably laughing his head off at my blunders, my venial and mortal mistakes. Or maybe he got bored and went off leaving me here on a brass bed turning, turning like Sordel, Sordello, which Sordello? Well he can do what he likes. I said: We all have weaknesses, but we have to focus on our strengths. I said: We're all writers, and in the end we all have to walk a long and rocky road. And from behind her long-suffering half-wit's face, María Canales looked at me as if she were weighing me up, and then she said: What a lovely thing to say, Father. And I looked back at her in surprise, partly because until then she had always called me Sebastián, like the rest of my literary friends, and partly because just at that moment the Mapuche maid appeared on the staircase holding the little boys. And that double apparition, the maid and little Sebastián along with María Canales's face and her calling me Father, as if she had suddenly given up the pleasant but trivial role she had been playing and taken on a new, far riskier role, that of penitent, that combination of sights conspired to make me lower my guard momentarily as they say (I suppose) in pugilistic circles, and momentarily enter a state akin to the joyful mysteries, those mysteries in which we all participate, of which we all partake, but which are unnameable, incommunicable, imperceptible from without, a state that brought on a feeling of dizziness, and nausea rising from my stomach, and closely resembled a combination of weeping, perspiration and tachycardia, and after leaving the welcoming home of our hostess it seemed to me this state had been provoked by the vision of the boy, my little namesake, who looked around with unseeing eyes as his hideous nanny carried him downstairs, his lips sealed, his eyes sealed, his innocent little body all sealed up, as if he didn't want to see or hear or speak, there in the midst of his mother's weekly party, in the presence of that joyous, carefree band of literati brought together by his mother each week. I don't know what happened next. I didn't pass out. I'm sure of that. Perhaps I resolved firmly not to attend any more of María Canales's soirées. I spoke with Farewell. He had already drifted so far away. Sometimes he talked about Pablo and it was as if Neruda were still alive. Sometimes he talked about Augusto, Augusto this, Augusto that, and hours if not days would pass before it became clear that he was referring to Augusto d'Halmar. To be frank, one could no longer have a conversation with Farewell. Sometimes I sat there looking at him and I thought: You old windbag, you old gossip, you old drunk, how are the mighty fallen. But then I would get up and fetch the things he asked for, trinkets, little silver or iron sculptures, old editions of Blest-Gana or Luis Orrego Luco that he was content simply to fondle. What has become of literature? I asked myself. Could the wizened youth be right? Could he be right after all? I wrote or tried to write a poem. In one line there was a boy with blue eyes looking through a window. Awful, ridiculous. Then I went back to María Canales's house. Everything was the same as before. The artists laughed, drank and danced, while outside, on the wide, empty avenues of Santiago, the curfew was in force. I didn't drink or dance. I just smiled beatifically. And thought. I thought how odd it was that, with all the racket and the lights, the house was never visited by a military or police patrol. I thought about María Canales, who by then had won a prize with her rather mediocre story. I thought about Jimmy Thompson, her husband, who was sometimes away for weeks or even months at a time. I thought about the boys, especially my little namesake, who was growing as if against his own will. One night I dreamt of Fr. Antonio, the curate of that church in Burgos, who had died cursing the art of falconry. I was in my house in Santiago, and Fr. Antonio appeared, looking very much alive, wearing a shiny cassock covered with clumsy darning, and without saying a word, he beckoned me to follow him. So I did. We went out into a paved courtyard bathed in moonlight. In the center was a leafless tree of indeterminate species. Fr. Antonio pointed it out to me, urgently, from the portico at the edge of the courtyard. Poor fellow, I thought, he's so old, but I looked carefully at the tree, and perched on one of its branches I saw a falcon. It's Rodrigo, it must be! I cried. Old Rodrigo, he looked so well, gallant and proud, elegantly perched on a branch, illuminated by Selene's rays, majestic and solitary. And then, as I was admiring the falcon, Fr. Antonio tugged at my sleeve and when I turned to look at him, I saw that his eyes were wide open and he was dripping with sweat and his cheeks and chin were trembling. And when he looked at me I realized that big tears were welling from his eyes, tears like cloudy pearls reflecting Selene's rays, and then Fr. Antonio's gnarled finger pointed to the portico and the arches on the other side of the courtyard, then to the moon or the moonlight, then the starless night sky, then the tree standing in the middle of that vast courtyard, and then he pointed to his falcon Rodrigo, and although he was trembling all the while, there was a certain method to this pointing. And I stroked his back, upon which a small hump had grown, but otherwise it was still a handsome back, like the back of an adolescent farm laborer or a novice athlete, and I tried to calm him, but no sound would come out of my mouth, and then Fr. Antonio began to cry inconsolably, so inconsolably that I felt a draught of cold air chilling my body and an inexplicable fear creeping into my soul, what was left of Fr. Antonio wept not only with his eyes but also with his forehead and his hands and his feet, hanging his head, a sodden rag under which the skin seemed to be perfectly smooth, and then, lifting his head, looking into my eyes, summoning all his strength, he asked me: Don't you realize? Realize what? I wondered, as Fr. Antonio melted away. It's the Judas Tree, he said between hiccups. His affirmation left no room for doubt or equivocation. The Judas Tree! I thought I was going to die right there and then. Everything stopped. Rodrigo was still perched on the branch. The paved courtyard was still illuminated by Selene's rays. Everything stopped. Then I began to walk towards the Judas Tree. At first I tried to pray, but I had forgotten all the prayers I ever knew. I walked. Under that immense night sky my steps made hardly a sound. When I had gone far enough I turned around and tried to say something to Fr. Antonio but he was nowhere to be seen. Fr.

Antonio is dead, I said to myself, by now he'll be in heaven or in hell. Or the Burgos cemetery, more likely. I walked. The falcon moved his head. One of his eyes was watching me. I walked. I'm dreaming, I thought. I'm asleep in my bed, in my house in Santiago. This courtyard or square looks Italian, but I'm not in Italy, I'm in Chile, I thought. The falcon moved his head. Now his other eye was watching me. I walked. Finally I reached the tree. Rodrigo seemed to recognize me. I raised my hand. The leafless branches of the tree seemed to be made of stone or papier-mâché. I raised my hand and touched a branch. Just then the falcon took flight, leaving me there alone. I'm lost, I cried out. I'm dead. When I got up the next morning a little tune was stuck in my head. From time to time I caught myself singing: The Judas Tree, the Judas Tree, during my classes, or as I walked in the garden, or when I took a break from my daily reading to make a cup of tea. The Judas Tree, the Judas Tree. One afternoon, as I was singing away to myself, I had a glimpse of what it meant: Chile itself, the whole country, had become the Judas Tree, a leafless, dead-looking tree, but still deeply rooted in the black earth, our rich black earth with its famous 40-centimeter earthworms. Then I went back to María Canales's house, and I think we must have had some kind of misunderstanding, I don't know, instead of enquiring about the novel she was writing, clearly a momentous enterprise, I asked after her sons and her husband, I said that life was much more important than literature, and she looked me in the eyes with that bovine face of hers and said she knew, she had always known that. My authority collapsed like a house of cards, while hers, or rather her supremacy, towered irresistibly. Feeling dizzy, I retired to my usual armchair to collect myself and weather the storm as best I could. That was the last time I attended one of her soirées. Months later a friend told me that during a party at María Canales's house one of the guests had gotten lost. He or she, my friend didn't know which, but I'll assume it was a he, was very drunk and went looking for the bathroom or the water closet, as some of my unfortunate countrymen still say. Perhaps he wanted to throw up, or just use the toilet, or splash some water on his face, but being so drunk, he got lost. Instead of taking the passage on the right, he took the one on the left, then he went along another passage, down some stairs, and before he knew it, he was in the basement, it was a huge house with a floor plan like a crossword puzzle. Anyhow, he went along various passages and opened various doors into rooms that were empty or had just a few packing cases in them, and spider webs the Mapuche maid never bothered to clear away. Finally he came to a passage that was narrower than the others and he opened one last door. He saw a kind of metal bed. He put on the light. On the bed was a naked man, his wrists and ankles tied. The man seemed to be asleep, but it was difficult to verify that impression, since he was blindfolded. The stray guest shut the door, feeling suddenly stone cold sober, and stealthily retraced his steps. When he got back to the sitting room he asked for a whiskey and then another and didn't say a word. Later, how much later I don't quite know, he told a friend, who then told my friend, who, much later on, told me. It was weighing heavily on my friend's conscience. Go in peace, I told him. Then I found out, from another friend, that the guest who had gotten lost was a playwright or maybe an actor, and that he had been down every one of the labyrinthine passages in María Canales and Jimmy Thompson's house, over and over until he arrived at that door at the end of a dimly lit corridor, and opened it and came across that body tied to a metal bed, abandoned in that basement, but alive, and the playwright or the actor shut the door stealthily, trying not to wake the poor man who was recuperating from his ordeal, and retraced his steps and returned to the party or the literary gathering, María Canales's soirée, without saying a word. And I also found out, years later, while watching clouds crumble, break apart and scatter in the Chilean sky, as Baudelaire's clouds would never do, that the guest who had gone astray in the deceptive corridors of that house on the outskirts of Santiago was a theorist of avant-garde theater, a theorist with a great sense of humor, who didn't panic when he lost his way, since as well as having a great sense of humor he was naturally curious, and when he realized he was lost in María Canales's basement, he wasn't afraid, in fact it appealed to the busybody in him, and he opened doors and even started whistling, and finally he came to the very last room at the end of the basement's narrowest corridor, lit by a single, feeble light bulb, and he opened the door and saw the man tied to the metal bed, blindfolded, and he knew the man was alive because he could hear him breathing, although he wasn't in good shape, for in spite of the dim light he saw the wounds, the raw patches, like eczema, but it wasn't eczema, the battered parts of his anatomy, the swollen parts, as if more than one bone had been broken, but he was breathing, he certainly didn't look like he was about to die, and then the theorist of avant-garde theater shut the door delicately, without making a noise, and started to make his way back to the sitting room, carefully switching off as he went each of the lights he had previously switched on. And months later, or maybe years later, another regular guest at those gatherings told me the same story. And then I heard it from another and another and another. And then democracy returned, the moment came for national reconciliation, and it was revealed that Jimmy Thompson had been one of the key agents of the DINA, and that he had used his house as a center for the interrogation of prisoners. The subversives were taken to the basement, where Jimmy interrogated them, extracting all the information he could, and then he sent them on to other detention centers. As a general rule, prisoners were not killed in Jimmy's house. It was meant to be just for interrogation, although there was the occasional death. It was also revealed that Jimmy had traveled to Washington and killed one of Allende's ex-ministers and a North American woman who happened to get in the way. And that he had organized the assassinations of exiled Chileans in Argentina, and even in Europe, that civilized continent, to which Jimmy had paid a brief visit with the diffidence befitting those born in the New World. All this came out. María Canales had known about it for a long time, of course. But she wanted to be a writer, and writers require the physical proximity of other writers. Jimmy loved his wife. María Canales loved her darling gringo. They had a pair of beautiful sons. Little Sebastián did not love his parents. But they were his parents! In her own dark way, the Mapuche maid loved María Canales and probably Jimmy as well. The men who worked for Jimmy didn't love him, but they probably had wives and children whom they loved in their own dark way. I asked myself the following question: If María Canales knew what her husband was doing in the basement, why did she invite guests to her house? The answer was simple: Because, normally, when she had a soirée, the basement was unoccupied. I asked myself the following question: Why then, on that particular night, did a guest who lost his way find that poor man? The answer was simple: Because, with time, vigilance tends to relax, because all horrors are dulled by routine. I asked myself the following question: Why didn't anyone say anything at the time? The answer was simple: Because they were afraid. I was not afraid. I would have been able to speak out, but I didn't see anything, I didn't know until it was too late. Why go stirring up things that have gradually settled down over the years? Later on Jimmy was arrested in the United States. He confessed. His confession implicated several Chilean generals. They took him out of jail and put him in a special witness protection program. As if the Chilean generals were mafia bosses! As if the Chilean generals had tentacles that could reach all the way to small towns in the American midwest to silence embarrassing witnesses! María Canales was all on her own. All her former friends, all the people who used to look forward to her parties cut her dead. One afternoon I went to see her. The curfew was a thing of the past, and it felt odd to be driving along those avenues on the outskirts, which were gradually changing. The house was no longer the same: all its former splendor, that untouchable, nocturnal splendor, had vanished. Now it was just an oversize house, with a neglected garden, completely overrun by towering weeds that had scaled the railings of the fence, as if to prevent the casual passerby from catching a glimpse of what was inside that building marked out for opprobrium. I parked beside the gate and stood outside for a while looking in. The windows were dirty and the curtains were drawn. A child's red bicycle was lying on the ground beside the steps up to the porch. I rang the bell. After a little while, the door opened. María Canales half opened the door and asked what I wanted. I said I wanted to talk with her. She hadn't recognized me. Are you a journalist? she asked. I'm

Father Ibacache, I said. Sebastián Urrutia Lacroix. For a few moments she seemed to be traveling back through time, then she smiled and stepped out, walked across the front garden to the gate and opened it. You're the last person I expected to see, she said. Her smile was not so different from the smile I remembered. It's so long ago, she said, as if reading my mind, but it feels like yesterday. We went into the house. There was not as much furniture as before, and the rooms, which I remembered as luminous, were now in a state of decrepitude comparable to that of the garden and seemed to be filled with a reddish dust, caught in a time warp where sad, remote, incomprehensible scenes were played over and over. My chair, the chair in which I used to sit, was still there. María Canales noticed me looking at it. Sit down, Father, she said, make yourself at home. I sat down without a word. Then I asked about her children. She told me they were spending a few days with some relatives. And they're well? I asked. Very well. Sebastián has shot up, if you saw him now you wouldn't recognize him. I asked about her husband. In the United States, she said. He lives in the United States now, she said. And how is he? I asked. Fine, I guess. With a movement that suggested weariness and disgust blended in equal parts, she drew up a chair, sat down and looked out through the dirty windows at the garden. She was rather fatter than before. And not as well dressed. I asked how she was, what she was doing. Don't you read the papers? she said, and then let out a vulgar snorting laugh, in which I detected a note of defiance that made me shudder. Her friends were gone, her money was gone, her husband had forgotten her and the children, nobody wanted to know her any more, but she was still there and she wasn't scared to laugh out loud. I asked about the Mapuche maid.

She went back to the south, she said, absently. And your novel, María, did you finish it? I whispered. I still haven't, Father, she said, lowering her voice like me. I rested my chin on my hand and thought for a while. I tried to think clearly, but couldn't. Meanwhile she was talking about the journalists who occasionally came to visit her, foreigners mostly. I want to talk about literature, she said, but they always get on to politics, Jimmy's work, my feelings at the time, the basement. I shut my eyes. Forgive her, I implored in silence, forgive her. Occasionally there are some Chilean or Argentine journalists, but not often. I make them pay for the interviews now. If they don't pay, I don't talk. But for all the gold in the world, I wouldn't tell them who used to come to my soirées. I promise you. Did you know about everything Jimmy was doing? Yes, Father. And do you repent? Like everyone else, Father. I felt I could hardly breathe. I got up and opened a window. The cuffs of my jacket got all dusty. Then she started telling me about the house. Apparently she didn't own the land, and the owners, Jews who had been in exile for over twenty years, were taking her to court. Since she had no money to hire a good lawyer, she was sure she would lose the case. The Jews were planning to demolish the house and build another from scratch. It's my house, said María Canales, and there'll be nothing left to remember it by. I looked at her sadly and said perhaps that was for the best, she was still young, she wasn't involved in any criminal proceedings, she could start over, with her children, somewhere else. And what about my literary career? she said with a defiant look. Use a nom de plume, a pseudonym, a nickname, for God's sake. She looked at me as if I had insulted her. Then she smiled: Do you want to see the basement? she said. I could have slapped her face, instead of which I sat there and shook my head several times. I shut my eyes. In a few months' time it will be too late, she said to me. By the tone of her voice and the warmth of her breath, I could tell she had brought her face very close to mine. I shook my head again. They're going to knock the house down. They'll rip out the basement. It's where one of Jimmy's men killed the Spanish UNESCO official. It's where Jimmy killed that Cecilia Sánchez Poblete woman. Sometimes I'd be watching television with the children, and the lights would go out for a while. We never heard anyone yell, the electricity just cut out and then came back. Do you want to go and see the basement? I stood up, took a few steps in that sitting room where our writers and painters, the artisans of our national culture, once used to gather, and shook my head. I must be off, María, I really have to go, I said to her. She burst out laughing uncontrollably. Or maybe I just imagined that. When we were standing on the porch (night was slowly beginning to fall), she took my hand, as if the thought of being left alone in that condemned house had suddenly scared her. I squeezed her hand and advised her to pray. I was very tired and didn't manage to put much conviction into my advice. I'm already praying as much as I can, she replied. Try, María, try, do it for your sons. She breathed in the air of outer Santiago, air that is the quintessence of dusk. Then she looked around, calm, serene, courageous in her own way, she looked at her house, her porch, the place where the cars used to park, the red bicycle, the trees, the garden path, the fence, the windows all shut except for the one I had opened, the stars twinkling far away, and she said, That's how literature is made in Chile. I nodded and left. While I was driving back into Santiago, I thought about what she had said. That is how literature is made in Chile, but not just in Chile, in Argentina and Mexico too, in Guatemala and Uruguay, in Spain and France and Germany, in green England and carefree Italy. That is how literature is made. Or at least what we call literature, to keep ourselves from falling into the rubbish dump. Then I started singing to myself again: The Judas Tree, the Judas Tree, and my car went back into the tunnel of time, back into time's giant meat grinder. And I remembered the day Farewell died. His funeral was discreet and orderly, as he would have wished. When I was left alone in his house, looking around the library, which was, in some mysterious way, the incarnation both of his absence and his presence, I asked his spirit (it was, of course, a rhetorical question) why things had turned out as they had for us. There was no reply. I went over to one of the huge bookcases and touched the spines of the books with my fingertips. There was a movement in a corner of the room. I jumped. But when I looked more closely, I saw that it was one of Farewell's faithful old crones who had fallen asleep. We left the house together, arm in arm. During the funeral procession, as we made our way through the refrigerated streets of Santiago, I asked what had become of Farewell. He's in the coffin, said some youths who were walking ahead of me. Idiots, I said, but the youths were gone, they had disappeared. Now I am the invalid. My bed is spinning, afloat on a swift-flowing river. If the waters were turbulent I would know that death was near. But the waters are just flowing quickly, so all hope is not yet lost. The wizened youth has been quiet for a long time now. He has given up railing against me and writers generally. Is there a solution? That is how literature is made, that is how the great works of Western literature are made. You better get used to it, I tell him. The wizened youth, or what is left of him, moves his lips, mouthing an inaudible *no*. The power of my thought has stopped him. Or maybe it was history. An individual is no match for history. The wizened youth has always been alone, and I have always been on history's side. I prop myself up on one elbow and look for him. All I can see are my books, the walls of my bedroom, a window in the midst of shadow and light. I could rise from this bed now and start living again, giving classes, writing reviews. I would like to review a book by one of the new French writers. But I haven't the strength. Is there a solution? One day, after Farewell's death, I went to his old estate, Là-bas, with a few friends, on a sort of sentimental journey, which I realized was a bad idea almost as soon as we got there. I went off for a walk through the fields where I had wandered as a young man. I looked for the farmers, but the sheds where they used to live were empty. An old woman was waiting to meet the friends who had come with me. I observed her from a distance, and when she headed for the kitchen, I followed and said hello to her from outside, through the window. She didn't even look at me. Later I found out she was half deaf, but the fact is she didn't even look at me. Is there a solution? One day, out of sheer boredom, I asked a young left-wing novelist if he knew how María Canales was getting on. The young man told me he had never met her. But you must have, you've been to her house, I said. He shook his head several times and changed the subject immediately. Is there a solution? Sometimes I come across farmers speaking another language. I stop them. I ask how things are on the land. But they tell me they don't work on the land. They tell me they work in factories or building sites in the city, they have never worked on the land. Is there a solution? Sometimes the earth shakes. The epicenter of the quake is somewhere in the north or the south, but I can hear the earth shaking. Sometimes I feel dizzy. Sometimes the quake goes on for longer than usual, and people take shelter in doorways or under stairs or they rush out into the street. Is there a solution? I see people running in the streets. I see people going into the Metro or into movie theaters. I see people buying newspapers. And sometimes it all shakes and everything stops for a moment. And then I ask myself: Where is the wizened youth? Why has he gone away? And little by little the truth begins to rise like a dead body. A dead body rising from the bottom of the sea or from the bottom of a gully. I can see its shadow rising. Its flickering shadow. Its shadow rising as if it were climbing a hill on a fossil planet. And then, in the half-light of my sickness, I see his fierce, his gentle face, and I ask myself: Am I that wizened youth? Is that the true, the supreme terror, to discover that I am the wizened youth whose cries no one can hear? And that the poor wizened youth is me? And then faces flash before my eyes at a vertiginous speed, the faces I admired, those I loved, hated, envied and despised. The faces I protected, those I attacked, the faces I hardened myself against and those I sought in vain.

And then the storm of shit begins.